Smoke Screen

AF418577

Karen Harbert

Copyright © 2020 Karen Harbert

All rights reserved. No part of this book may be used or reproduced in any manner whatsoever without written permission, except in the case of brief quotations embodied in critical articles and reviews.

This is a work of fiction. Any similarity to real persons, living or dead is coincidental.

ISBN:

DEDICATION

For all the good friends and wonderful dogs who have made these books possible, and my thanks to the fans who keep me writing!

CONTENTS

ACKNOWLEDGMENTS

Smoke Screen was the title of a mystery by Dick Francis, probably the author I most admire. Smoke Screen was also the name of the grandsire of my first Cardigan.

A major Tucson-area brush fire really was caused by a father-to-be shooting an explosive target at a gender-reveal event, and we have just learned that one of the major California fires now burning was caused the same way. I guess you just can't fix stupid.

Thanks, as always, to the team that helps make these books possible: Marilyn Boissonneault and Pat Nelson, my eagle-eyed proofreaders, and Jovana Shirley who turns my manuscripts into expertly done e-books. And, of course, Tim Gates, who turns my half-baked concepts into stunning covers. In this case, the cover was already done and the book nearing its end when I had that 3:00 AM inspiration that resulted in my asking him to revisit and revise it.

CHAPTER ONE
(*Tuesday, October 8*)

It had been a long day and as I walked in the front door and through into the dining room I could see the red message indicator on the phone blinking. The actual answering machine was in my home office; this one was connected to the Caller ID and only displayed the phone number. I glanced at it and the area code looked familiar but the number wasn't one I frequently called, or that called here often enough that I would recognize it. Possibly club business; I'd check it after I saw to the dogs. Monty had permanent house privileges these days since his grandson, Dragon, had reached maturity. It wasn't wise to leave two adult, intact, male dogs unsupervised when some trivial provocation could cause them to forget their manners. In plain, unvarnished terms, I wasn't going to risk a dog fight between my two champion stud dogs.

My beloved Monty was American, Mexican and Canadian Champion Brookside Merry Monarch, and also American CDX (Companion Dog Excellent) and Canadian UD (Utility Dog); obedience titles that proved he had brains as well as beauty. His grandson, American and Canadian Champion Brookside Flaming Dragon, had earned the CD, or Companion Dog title, earlier this year in both our country and Canada, showing he was also on his way to higher levels of canine obedience.

I sent Monty out into the small, fenced front yard, dropped my briefcase in the office and went to change out of professional suit, nylons and heels. I had just buttoned a casual shirt when the phone rang. There was no phone in the bedroom so I trotted, barefoot, down the hall to the office. I wasn't quick enough and the answering machine kicked in again. I waited through the message ("I can't get to the phone right now and the dogs aren't tall enough to reach it, so please leave a message. If you're not a telemarketer I'll return your call.")

"Jennifer, this is Charlene. You're lucky Mother didn't call and get that rude message. Please call me immediately; it's urgent."

If Mother was having a serious health problem, I'm sure she would have said so. Nothing else concerning my family was urgent enough to make me jump through any flaming hoops for them. It was only a few months since my mother had almost let me get killed by her greedy 'spiritual advisor' who hoped to get his hands on the significant assets I had inherited from my late husband, Kent Wyler.

I'd been remarried now for three years, to Royal Canadian Mounted Police Superintendent Alexander MacLeod, a 'world renowned' forensics expert, author of two books used in the law enforcement academies of a good many jurisdictions on both sides of our international border. He taught his subjects at the University of Lethbridge, his own home base, and occasionally gave short courses in other parts of each of our countries.

Despite his impressive credentials, my mother considered a policeman socially beneath her notice, while Charlene's husband, Donald, running for the U.S. Congress, thought it would help his campaign if his wife's sister weren't married to 'an alien.' I didn't think anything they considered urgent could possibly be of interest to me. And, since I had worked late and it was three hours later in Atlanta, it should be too late to call anyone back east if I just pretended I hadn't been home yet for her second call.

I brought the other dogs in from the back yard: Monty's grandson, Dragon, and Misty, American/Canadian Champion Brookside Mistletoe; a granddaughter of Dragon's other grandsire, the incomparable English and American Champion Blakeleigh Excalibur, and hopefully in whelp to Dragon. The numbers had diminished here since Champion Brookside Poppycock had lost a litter in early summer and had to be spayed. Poppy had gone home with my elderly neighbor, Marcus Todd, retired U.S. marshal. It was time to bring a new puppy into the household so I'd have something to show again. Alex's darling, Champion Belladonna, had puppies on the way – also hopefully – and maybe I should bring one of them home.

I had thawed a salmon steak for my dinner and was looking forward to poaching it in wine and topping it with a dill-Hollandaise sauce accompanied by a green salad.

Alex's time zone was an hour later than mine so I called him before I fed the dogs and started my own dinner.

"No news yet, lass, Belladonna isn't showing, of course, but her appetite seems bottomless so I'm hopeful. Tabby will palpate at four weeks and you'll be the next to know." That was his veterinarian, Dr.

Tabitha Bowman; when Alex had called her over to introduce her at our wedding ('Tabby, over here') I had looked around for a cat.

Belladonna had been bred to Alex's Champion Tobermory and was due two weeks later than Misty. "I'll keep my fingers crossed; we need new puppies."

"That reminds me, young Jamie phoned yesterday to tell me they'd planted a peach tree, and he wanted a new puppy too."

If I hadn't known what that oblique reference meant it would have mystified me, but I remembered the conversation a couple of years ago when the dog that had helped to raise his nephews was very old and mostly slept all the time. Jamie and I had a heart-to-heart conversation about the lifespans of dogs and I'd suggested having old Briar cremated when the time came, and planting a fruit tree in his memory. "So they finally lost the old dog."

"After a very long and happy life. Jamie's likely to pester us for a puppy. I don't think it would be wise to give them a half-sister of Frodo to found his breeding program."

"Probably not with Toby also closely related, but we have several other options. Didn't you tell me that Melanie was also going to breed Ruthie?" Alex had named his first Cardigan litter from the Lord of the Rings trilogy. Melanie Vollmer had asked for the remaining puppy in that litter, Brookside Ringwraith, called 'Ruthie,' and she had been bred to Melanie's own champion who was totally unrelated to the rest of our line.

"Aye, and Myrna Watson plans to breed her lovely Haida, to the boys' Frodo. That litter would also be too closely related for them."

The breeding of relatives, 'line breeding,' or in the case of close relatives, 'inbreeding,' was a time-tested system meant to concentrate the best features of animals highly efficient in whatever characteristics were most important to their breed; whether beef, or milk, or egg-laying, or race track speed. Experienced breeders did this cautiously; you could just as easily concentrate the genetic landfill material as the treasure chest. If a young boy was about to embark on a breeding program, we wanted to give him the best possible start. Not that there was much genetic junk in the pedigrees of our dogs, but over half a century ago a dreaded recessive gene was concentrated in a few of the dogs left in our breed in Britain after two World Wars, and entire kennels were wiped out by Progressive Retinal Atrophy. In the late 1990's the genetic marker for the disease was identified. I helped in the efforts to submit first blood samples, and then cheek swabs to the research center, and now all of our dogs could be cleared of that scourge by a simple test, and from then on, by pedigree.

"And there's one more possibility; Mandy's Bonita was bred to her Brewster."

"Hmm, maybe, lass, we should consider a round-robin trade with these puppies so each of us ends up with one that's not so closely related to the dogs at home."

"Excellent idea. We owe Barb a pup from Melanie's litter for helping to finish Ruthie, but we can float all these pedigrees around and see who's interested in what."

"Soo, with that settled, tell me there are no serial murderers lurking around until I get down there."

We had been contacted by the Pima County Attorney's Office with a request for depositions in the case of two children that had been found dead in a storage shed after my boss had sent me to check on their welfare. I was to meet with the attorney when I arrived next week; Alex would have his interview when he met me in Tucson next month.

"Not a one. Oh, and my sister left two messages telling me to contact her, that it was 'urgent,' and I've ignored both."

"Probably a wise move after our last experience with them; let's hope they don't have another plan to have me assassinated this time."

"If Mother was having a health crisis I'm sure Charlene would have said so; any other emergency of theirs has nothing to do with us. I told you before, I'm delighted with your family; I don't need any further dealings with mine."

The phone rang again as I was melting butter to sauté the salmon. When I let it go to the answering machine I heard my mother's strident voice. "Jennifer Hawley, answer this phone! I know you're home by now and we've been calling for a couple of hours."

I sighed and picked up the phone, "Mother, I'm just home from work, it was a long day, I have to feed the dogs, and I'm trying to fix my own dinner."

"Well, your sister needs your help, so just put your family before your animals for a change."

Why? I wondered. My Superdog, Monty, had put himself in peril protecting me more than once in the past, while my family had put me in danger without a second thought. Oh, well. "Mother, please tell me the emergency; I really have to take care of things here."

"You were on the phone with someone else for at least half an hour."

"My husband."

"That fortune hunter! This is more important. Donald has to go to Tucson for an important congressional assignment. You have a house there and he needs a place to stay."

"Mother, as you can see, we're not in Tucson right now."

"Just send me the address, and the key, it doesn't matter if you're there or not."

"Well, yes it does matter   We don't just mail out keys to our house. And Donald hasn't even been elected yet."

"His congressional backers need his intervention in a project that's important enough that Donald mustn't fail them."

"What on earth has that to do with us, or our house?"

"It's *your* house; it has nothing to do with your so-called husband."

"We don't agree, and anyway, I'm not mailing a key to Donald. I'm sure his backer can afford a hotel."

"Donald needs a local residence where he can meet people, hold confidential meetings, and do some entertaining. He needs to show that he has local connections."

"Mother, I don't know what kind of a scam Donald may be running, but he's not going to do it from our house."

"He's not doing any such thing! He's certain to win the election in November, but he won't be seated until after the first of the year, and even then there's a slight delay in drawing his congressional salary. His backers want him in Tucson immediately after the election to use his influence as an elected congressman in a very large and important construction project."

"What project?" I tried to keep on top of Southern Arizona news and I'd like to form my own opinion of the merits of Donald's project before lending our support.

"Donald said it's confidential, with very delicate negotiations."

"Well, you can have Donald call me and explain it. Alex and I will be in Tucson ourselves shortly, so if we approve of his plans we might let him come to the house for a meeting while we're there. But that's as far as I'm willing to go."

"Donald has to go there very soon. And he doesn't need you there; you'd probably just try to upstage him again the way you did here."

"Alex and I come with the house. Tell Donald to take it or leave it."

"I just don't understand you. You were raised to respect your family, and you certainly weren't raised to be this selfish."

I wanted to remind her of the last time she had told me to put my family ahead of my own interests and almost got me killed; as if that would have done any good. "Mother, I really have to take care of all our dinners. Have Donald call me himself if he wants to discuss it further. Now goodnight." And I disconnected the phone.

I should let Alex know about my mother's audacious request – more like a demand – but it would be pointless to call him again tonight, and I didn't need a second opinion as to whether or not I should keep my entire family at arm's length.

I fed the dogs and my thoughts turned again to how diminished our numbers were. Maybe for distraction tonight I should print out all the potential pedigrees of the litters on the way, something to take my mind off of my mother's attempt to insert Charlene's husband into our comfortable, secluded and peaceful Tucson home.

I should have known I hadn't heard the end of this. When I got home the next afternoon there were two messages on my answering machine from my sister, and the phone rang again before I had even changed my clothes. I checked the caller ID and it was the same number as yesterday's; my sister's as I now knew. I picked it up, "What, Charlene?"

An unfamiliar voice asked, "Is this Ms. Jennifer Hawley?"

"No, it certainly isn't. I'm Mrs. MacLeod. And who are you?"

"I'm the au pair for Congressman and Mrs. Donald Roth."

"So?"

"I've been tasked with arranging for Congressman Roth's trip to Tucson. I understand he will be staying in a house you own or rent and he will need the address and a key."

"Donald isn't Congressman Roth; he hasn't even been elected yet, and if he would like to visit us in our Tucson home, he can call and ask me himself."

"He's a very busy man."

"I'm a very busy woman," and I didn't even bother to say goodbye, I just hung up the phone.

The next call was from my sister. "Jennifer, I can't believe how hostile you've become toward your family and your responsibilities to us."

You think? After my family was willing to overlook an attempt to first annul my marriage, and then murder me? "Charlene, I have no idea what Donald is up to, but we are not mailing him a key to our house. If he wants to visit, he can make the effort to talk to me himself and tell me what's so important."

"Well, he's at a campaign meeting tonight, so he asked me to arrange it."

"Charlene, we'll both be in Tucson late next week. If Donald would like to meet with someone at our house, while we're present, have him call me. Himself. I'm tired of phone calls from Mother, and you, and even your live-in nanny; I refuse to discuss this with anyone else except the Congressional wannabe who wants something from me. From us. I'm also tired of my family refusing to acknowledge my husband. That's my last word on the subject with anyone else but Donald."

CHAPTER TWO
(*Friday, October 18, Tucson*)

This was just about the best time of year in Tucson. The searing heat of early summer was gone, as was the stifling humidity of the summer monsoon. Nights were cool and even daytime temperatures were pleasant – as long as you're comfortable at somewhere around ninety degrees.

My young friend, Mandy, was house-sitting overnight with Monty, Misty and Dragon. When we came back here in November for the dog shows Dragon would compete for Best of Breed and Herding Group placements, and Monty would compete for a new title in the Utility ring. Monty was a top show dog who had won Best in Show in both our country and Canada, but his tenth birthday would be celebrated here with a good steak when Alex and I finally came over for the shows next month. Pregnant Misty would come along just in case we had to deliver her litter here instead of at home in semi-rural San Diego County.

I had flown over this morning so I could meet with the County Attorney today to give a signed deposition regarding our discovery of the remains of the two children Alex and I had come here to investigate some months earlier. The father and his girlfriend had somehow caused or concealed the deaths of the children while the frantic mother in San Diego had been trying to get them back. Now, the prosecuting attorney was leading me through the events of that afternoon with a recorder running. We had already covered the events leading up to our department director asking me to take a trip over here to check on the welfare of the two preschool children.

"So when you got to the house...?"

"The next-door neighbor told us she had never seen children at the house, and then, almost as an afterthought, that she thought they had moved away leaving their garbage in that shed because when the wind blew from that direction, it was very stinky. We went to the house to knock on the doors although we were already pretty certain that no one was there. Another gust of wind blew through the yard while we were there and my husband recognized the odor of decomposition."

"How did he recognize that, as opposed to, well, garbage?"

"He teaches forensics at the University of Lethbridge."

"And where is that?"

"In Alberta, Canada."

"So will he be available to testify?"

"He can be if we're able to get enough notice to be sure we don't have any conflicts of our own."

"We estimate the trial will take about two weeks. If you could make yourselves available during those two weeks it would be very helpful."

"Yes, but we're both employed in our own home towns and that would use a great deal of our vacation time on the off chance that you're ready for us." Of course the actual days either of us testified, plus travel days on each side, would be paid leave for each of us since we were involved in official duties, but I didn't have to tell the attorney that.

She continued taking me through our calls to 911, the police response, and finally the media clusterfuck – although neither of us used that word – when I called all the local news outlets and gave live interviews with the caseworker's manager and supervisor fuming on the sidelines.

"So your husband opened that storage shed...?"

"No, absolutely not. One of the things he teaches is how to preserve a crime scene. The first police officer on the scene forced open the doors even while my husband was suggesting that a warrant might be required."

"Hmm, the police report just notes that he opened the door, it says nothing about having to force it."

"I assume you'll have him testify under oath."

I couldn't help but notice that this prosecutor showed no recognition of Alex's name or status as the author of texts on both fingerprints, and preserving crime scenes, which were widely used in officer training. There had to be someone in law enforcement who hadn't heard of RCMP Superintendent Alexander MacLeod, we just hadn't encountered very many.

It took another hour, but she had finally wrung out everything I remembered from that miserable day, and I was glad I had taken copious notes at the time. With no crosstown freeways as we were accustomed to in southern California, it was almost an hour's drive from the County Attorney's office downtown back to our secluded home in the Tanque Verde Valley in the far northeast part of the county.

I pulled a halibut steak from the freezer when I got to the house. It was delicious with a sauce of pickled radishes accompanied by zucchini with crumbled blue cheese. I ate in front of the television watching what had been the lead story for the last couple of days; the attempts by an out-of-state developer to gain permits for a nearly thirty-thousand-home subdivision in a small town south of the interstate and not far from pristine Kartchner Caverns, a spectacular living cave system only discovered late in the last century by a couple of amateur cavers from the University of Arizona. There were serious concerns about what a development of that size would do to the groundwater table for the riparian areas of one of the last free-flowing rivers in southern Arizona, as well as any possible impact on the caves themselves.

A talking head from a Phoenix-area station was interviewing a representative of the developer. "Those enviros are out to stifle any growth in the state. They'll put water out in the desert to encourage illegals to flood the country, but they want to stop us from building homes for the citizens who were born here!"

"Harsh words, and I don't think they're the same organizations."

"It doesn't make any difference; our project is perfect for that hill country. Our Tuscan villas will blend beautifully into the landscape."

"You said those homes would be for people born here, but aren't you also expecting significant sales to snowbirds from Canada?"

"If they can afford a second home, why not?"

"No, my point was that you said people born here."

"Well, the Canadians are..." and he seemed at loss for a word. I was sure the word on the tip of his tongue had been 'white.' "Um, they're like us; they speak our language. But who buys them is beside the point; we're creating a dream out there where there's nothing now but desert. Our development will have schools, parks, recreation centers."

"Some people contend that the ground water available can't support the seventy thousand anticipated new residents. Others have concerns that the area is lacking in basic resources such as medical and hospital services, and urban amenities, and it's over an hour to get to Tucson."

"If we build this, the services will move out there."

There were a few more questions, but I definitely got the point of why we should keep ourselves informed about what was going on locally. Our neighbor, Augustin had told me, 'Jennifer, you and Alexander should be aware that there may be protests about this project while you're here. The protesters will probably try to disrupt the bicycle race, which may interfere with your weekend as well.'

I was a registered voter in California, Alex was Canadian, neither of us had any standing as far as voting on anything to do with this development, but it was good to stay informed. I knew the area of that planned community and I had to agree that I didn't think the local area could support such a grand scheme. I was sure we'd all talk it over when Alex and I were here next month.

The events we were coming over for were the annual Tucson dog shows, eight of them over two weekends. The first set of shows at the Rillito River Park was outdoors, and it almost always rained. The later four shows were at the Pima County Fairgrounds, where it could also rain, but our breed was usually scheduled for indoor rings at least half of the days. That was usually the same weekend as the Tucson bicycle race that snarled traffic around town for most of Saturday, but thankfully, this year the bicycle race would be a week later because Thanksgiving fell later than usual.

I had taken the advice of one of our top professional handlers and started showing Monty's grandson, Dragon, as a Special, while brushing up Monty's obedience for the Utility Dog title. With two litters on the way – hopefully – we should have young dogs to show in the next year.

CHAPTER THREE
(*Monday, October 21*)

I got back home on Saturday and went to work today. I had to report on my deposition to both my own boss and our District Attorney, Damaris Colton. My boss, department director Dr. Wendell Pierce, had asked me to take a paid trip to our house in Tucson this past spring to find out what I could about the children. Damaris was interested in the case because one of her staff had been to court on behalf of the mother who was trying to get her children back. I gave Wendell a telephone briefing when I got to work this morning. His wife, Amber, and Damaris, would get the full story over lunch tomorrow.

I was looking forward to tomorrow's lunch with those two very good friends when I got home, but my good mood evaporated when I saw the blinking light on the phone with what I recognized as my mother's number. After I changed clothes I went into my office and poked the playback button. "Jennifer, call me immediately. Donald has to be in Tucson in two weeks and he needs access to your house there."

I could be sure that she'd keep calling until I answered the phone, so I ignored that message and let the dogs in. Misty wasn't giving away anything about her pregnancy, but just over four weeks had gone by, and I had an appointment after work tomorrow with my vet, Dr. Sandra Spaulding, to examine her and give me a professional opinion.

I was digging in the freezer for a leftover for tonight's dinner when the phone rang again. I picked up the kitchen phone and of course, it was my mother. "Jennifer Hawley, I told you to call me immediately."

"Mother, I have priorities of my own. And I've said several times that I won't discuss Donald's use of our house with anyone except him. I've heard from you, from Charlene, and even from Donald's live-in baby sitter. My answer hasn't changed: Donald can call me himself."

"He's very busy. These are the closing weeks of his campaign and his project in Tucson is of vital importance to some of his important backers."

"Mother, the last time we were involved with one of Donald's important backers the guy planned to kill us."

"Oh, don't be such a drama queen. Reverend Gentry had his faults, but he wasn't a murderer."

I wanted to tell her of Amber's offer to bake her one of her famous Egyptian cakes, "For the Queen of Denial." It wouldn't have done any good; my mother had her own reality. "Mother, tell Donald he has to call and discuss it with me. That's my final word." This time I hung up before she could.

When the phone rang again I checked the caller ID and it was that same almost familiar number from two weeks ago. Now I recognized it as my sister's. I picked it up and when that unfamiliar voice asked "Is this Jennifer Hawley?" I simply disconnected it again.

I had fed the dogs and warmed my own dinner when the phone rang yet again. This time the display read only 'Wireless Caller.' I let it go to the answering machine and soon heard a male voice yelling at me from the other room. "Goddammit, Jennifer, answer this phone. My people have been calling you all night."

"And good evening to you too, Donald. It's about time you bothered to call me yourself."

"I don't have time for small talk; I'm at a campaign event tonight. Our fund raising dinner is just wrapping up and I'll be addressing my constituents."

"Bully for you; you interrupted my dinner. It's getting cold; get to the point."

"I need the family house in Tucson. I'm flying out there the day after the election for an important meeting. I need you to mail me the key."

"Donald, where did you get that 'family house' alternative reality factoid? It's my house; mine and my husband's."

"We're family! You don't live there, it's your vacation home, and your sister's family has a right to spend time in it."

"Donald, your last important meeting resulted in your family's spiritual advisor's attempt to eliminate both of us."

"Your mother is right; you have an overactive imagination."

My entire family was in denial about that whole debacle and it didn't look like I was going to ever change their minds. "Tell me what you want, Donald, before my dinner gets so cold that I won't want to listen to anything you have to say."

"I'm flying to Tucson the morning after the election. Some of my backers will be meeting with me. I need a house where we can meet in private and where I can entertain."

"I'll be there that day so you can have your meeting, but you won't be staying at the house or holding political rallies there. If you need a facility for that, we can recommend a couple of nice hotels."

"I need privacy; just put off your trip for a few days."

"Donald, you really don't get it. It's *our house*, not a short-term rental or a time share. It's not available for your entertaining pleasure. You may hold your meeting there during the day while I'm there to protect our interests, and then you can go to a hotel."

"Why can't I stay there? I need to make it look like I have a local presence."

"I'll put you in touch with a nice real estate agent who can help you with an actual short-term rental."

"Why are you being so obstructive? Don't you realize how much it can be to your advantage to have the goodwill of a congressman in your family?"

"Donald, your definition of family seems to be rather one-sided since your live-in baby sitter…

"She's our *au-pair*."

"Whatever label you give her, she has twice referred to me as Jennifer Hawley. My name is MacLeod"

"That's your mother's fault."

"She's your employee."

His voice took on a whine, "You know how difficult it can be to argue with her; she always has to have the last word."

"Well, you've heard my last word on the subject of our house. Goodnight, I'm going to reheat my dinner."

I had just reheated my leftover when the phone rang again. This time the display showed Alex's number in Alberta so I left the chicken in the microwave. "Alex, darling, yours is the only phone call I still would have taken tonight."

"I noticed that your phone was having a busy hour or so."

"My mother, and then my brother-in-law. The Donald wants our house for his important meetings, and he needs to give the impression that he has a local presence for entertaining. I entertained him just long enough to make our position really, really clear, and then I put my dinner back in the microwave.”

“Uh, oh; is it still warm?”

“It’s still in there. I told Donald he could hold his super-important meeting at the house the day after I get there, I’ll meet you at the airport that morning, and then you can meet with the County Attorney the next day. Trust me, Donald will not be staying at the house, and he’ll have to provide his own transportation. I’ll give him a couple of hours for his meeting and that’s all.”

“Then we’ll have a pleasant holiday and hope for success at the shows.”

CHAPTER FOUR
(Monday, November 4 – Wednesday, November 6)

I arrived late Monday afternoon with the dogs. Donald had arrived ahead of me and was fretting in a room at the Hilton, as several messages on my answering machine indicated. Why he had started calling every half hour from noon on when he had been told that I had a seven-hour drive was a mystery, but here were six identical messages telling me to call him as soon as I arrived. Like hell.

I called Alex and let him know I had arrived safely. His flight into Tucson would arrive tomorrow morning, and none too soon. When I finally called Donald, after making the dogs comfortable and adjusting the house temperature, he was impatient and fairly testy.

"You know how important this is to me; why didn't you call me back as soon as you got here?"

"Donald, this isn't necessarily as important to me. I agreed to let you have a meeting here tomorrow, but this is still our house…"

"Your house. Your mother assures us that your alien husband has no standing."

"In your dreams, Donald. Both of our names are on the title to all of our properties…"

"Are you crazy, Jennifer? You're allowing that fortune hunter equal equity in all of your extremely valuable assets. You're just asking to be double-crossed."

"Donald, it's actually none of your business if we put the dogs' names on the titles."

"Well, of course it is; you can make a substantial contribution to my success and you shouldn't sneeze at the influence a congressman in the family can have on your own career."

Yeah, right. "No thanks, Donald. We've agreed to let you have a meeting here tomorrow and that's the extent of our involvement in whatever scheme you're working on."

"Well, I'll be there at ten in the morning and my constituents will be there about half an hour later. We require a private place to meet, and it wouldn't be amiss for you to offer refreshments, and maybe lunch."

"I'll give your request serious consideration." I didn't tell him that Alex's flight would arrive roughly halfway through his high-level meeting and I would have backup if he tried to pressure me into anything.

So Donald rolled up to my door about nine-forty-five, pushed his way in through the front door, and said, "Now show me around this place."

"Donald, this is our kitchen/great room and the dining room table where you can hold your meeting."

"Not acceptable; we need private quarters."

"Tough. Your hotel may be more suitable."

In the end, Donald settled for what I was willing to concede, but then his political contacts arrived and immediately started making their way through my house to decide what area might be suitable for their meeting. Both were dressed in suits, the older of them seemed to be in charge, while the other, carrying the briefcase, looked more like a bodyguard in a suit that was just a little too tight. I was quietly seething as they took themselves on a tour of my house, but thought I'd bide my time until Alex was here to offer reinforcements. Both of Donald's 'backers' struck me as slightly bruising as far as their interactions with anyone who disagreed with them.

My theory was borne out when I overheard the tough-looking guy say to Donald, "Hey, that broad's quite a looker. You getting any?"

"She's my wife's sister."

"Keep it in the family, I always say."

"My wife couldn't make it here; the children, you know. Her sister is here to act as hostess for me."

"I'll take some of her hospitality when we're done with our meeting, but for now, get her out of here. Send her shopping or something."

"I was going to ask her to make lunch for us."

"She can do that when she gets back, meanwhile, I'll get her out of here. Hey, Cupcake..."

I definitely didn't answer to 'Cupcake,' and I ignored him. The next thing I knew he had grabbed my arm. "I'm talking to you."

I pulled my arm away, "That's not my name."

"Like I care, get outta here, go shopping, or whatever you broads do, but we need privacy."

"I hadn't planned on leaving quite this soon."

"Well, your plans have changed so grab your purse and get moving."

There were two goons, and I could expect as much help from Donald as when the 'family spiritual advisor' had decided I would be most useful to his 'ministry' if I were deceased, with my mother as my heir.

"Well, I'll just have to check something on the computer before I go."

"What's your problem with plain English? We're having a private meeting in your brother's house and you're persona au gratin, or whatever. So go, already. Where's your purse?"

"In the bedroom. Take your hands off of me."

"I'll just walk you there to get it." He tried to keep his hand on my elbow but I brushed it off.

I had left my bag in the master bedroom and I didn't want any of these creeps in my personal space, but he wasn't willing to give up. "So, you've got your stuff in the master bedroom? I guess our boy Donald is getting some after all. Maybe he'll share. But right now, git."

"You'll have to wait while I load the dogs; I'm not leaving them here when I'm not home."

"What? You brought a bunch of dogs to our congressman's house? He's sure not as fussy as I'd be."

I went around to the laundry room where the dogs were in the indoor runs, leashed the three of them, and took them out to the motor home, with the goon on my tail every step of the way. He was so close to me that Monty growled, and the guy said, "If that mutt makes a wrong move, I'll break its neck."

If I hadn't been heading for the airport to bring Alex back to the house I think I would have kept going far enough to be out of their sight and then called the Sheriff. I really wanted to make an issue of the guy's behavior to me in my own home, but not with two-and-a-half against one, with my dogs possibly vulnerable; especially pregnant Misty. I'd be back here in an hour and a half with reinforcements.

As I walked the dogs past the great room to the front door I heard the goon-in-charge say, "Donny, boy, we don't care what it takes, you get that so-called expert in the Fish and Game Department to change his story and get our permit issued. You hear me? What the fuck business does some fish guy have turning down our permit?"

I loaded the dogs into the motorhome with the under-goon looking on, and he said, "He lets you drive his Mercedes? You must be as hot as you look."

It took a lot of will power to simply ignore him, but I got into the driver's seat and drove down to the airport. I figured I was nearly an hour early but on checking the flight schedule on my phone I saw that Alex's flight was almost half an hour ahead of schedule. The temperature was comfortable and the airport had been in the process of converting to solar power so there was a large area of the parking lot now under shade with solar panels above. I cracked the windows, locked the motor home, and went inside the terminal. My airline app was right; Alex's plane was on its final approach and within twenty minutes he was on his way down the ramp.

"Alex, you have no idea how glad I am to see you today."

"Does that imply seduction before suppertime?"

"No, it means there are a couple of goons sitting in our house right now who think it's Donald's house, and who seem to think I'm a hostess who should be hospitable."

"Are they aware that your husband might object?"

I smiled for the first time this morning. "Alex, my darling, they have no idea I'm coming back to the house with you. They think they've sent me out shopping for a couple of hours."

As we set out back to the house he asked, "Describe them for me, will you?"

"They don't look or sound like they're from around here. One of them looks older than either of us, one looks younger, but they both look like more muscle than intellect. As I left the house I heard the one who seems to be in charge tell Donald to get someone in Fish and Wildlife to change his opinion and get their permit issued."

"Any idea what kind of permit they're talking about?"

"Not a clue, but the way they hustled me out of the house it can't be something they want witnesses to."

He pulled out his phone while I was talking and punched in a number. "Detective Moreno, it's Alex MacLeod. Are you on duty, or off? Off, marvelous. How would you like to meet us at the house for a beer? But first we might have some vermin to pitch out. Wait until you see us pull in with the little motor home, give us about five minutes inside and then just walk right in without using the doorbell. Aye, vermin. Some rats showed up this morning to have a talk with Jennifer's brother-in-law and all but threw her out of her own home. Thanks, we're about twenty minutes out." When he signed off he had a very smug look on his face.

When I parked the motor home back in the shade of the spacious carport Alex said, "You go in first, but leave the dogs here for now. I'll follow a few seconds behind you; just long enough to give them time to do something that will make us angry."

I smiled. I was going to enjoy this. I let myself back in and as soon as he heard the door open the under-goon strode into the entry.

"What are you doing back here already?"

"I finished my errand."

"Well we haven't finished our business. Go out and get us a pizza. Two pizzas, big ones. Never mind drinks, our Donald has a full wine cooler."

"Actually, that's my wine cooler and you weren't invited for lunch."

He took a step closer and grabbed my arm, and I smelled alcohol on his breath. Just then Alex came through the door carrying his duffel bag.

"Who the hell are you?" Goon demanded.

"I should be asking the questions," Alex told him. He had dropped his bag and pulled out his badge in one fluid move, and with his thumb firmly over the RCMP, it simply said Police. "I'll see some identification now, if you don't mind."

"Yeah, I mind. We're having a business meeting in my friend's house, it's private, and we sent this broad out to go shopping."

Alex turned to me, "Jennifer, is this a friend of yours?"

"Absolutely not; Donald didn't even introduce them. They marched in here like they owned the place and started giving me orders."

The goon-in-charge came out of the dining area, took in the situation at a glance, and said, "We're all done here, Dwayne," and headed for the front door, but Alex was in the way.

"Not quite yet," he said, "This fellow had his hands on my wife. I asked for identification, and I haven't seen it yet."

"I'm sure it's a misunderstanding; we're here for a meeting with the homeowner, our business is concluded and we'll be on our way."

I had shifted my position so I was near the door and I sneaked a glance out the tall window next to it just as Deputy Gabriel Moreno's pickup truck coasted to a stop. I moved away from the door and when Alex glanced at me I nodded.

He slipped his badge back into his pocket and said, "I find it mystifying that you had a meeting with the homeowner, but you sent her away."

"What are you talking about?"

"I mean that this is our home, and you appear to be misusing our hospitality. Oh, good afternoon, Detective Moreno, we're so glad you could stop by. I'm not sure whether or not this qualifies as a home invasion, but these gentlemen did not introduce themselves to my wife earlier, and haven't produced identification when I came home and asked for it."

"Are they trespassing, Superintendent MacLeod?"

"Once they refused to identify themselves to me, in my own home, yes, I would say so."

Gabriel turned to the two men with his own badge in his hand. "So if you aren't here for a meeting with Superintendent and Mrs. MacLeod, why did you come here?"

"We were meeting with the new congressman, Donald Roth. We understood this was his house."

"Since it's not, I think it's time you showed your identification."

They reluctantly pulled out their wallets. Gabriel read the names aloud, "Dwayne Maguirk and Lawrence DeLuca, both of Washington, DC." He pulled out a small notebook and copied down all of their information and then used his phone to take pictures of their ID's. "Did you wish to press charges, Mrs. Macleod?"

"No, not this time, not unless they show up at our house again."

"Then you two are free to leave, and be sure you don't come back to this address."

I had been waiting for my cowardly brother-in-law to make his appearance and smooth over the problem. When he didn't, I told Gabriel, "He's not a congressman yet; he won an election but won't be seated until next year. I think it's time he joined us." But Donald wasn't at my dining table, nor in the living room. He was nowhere in sight so I went looking. I found him stretched out on the king-sized bed in the master bedroom – with his shoes on. "Donald! What in the hell are you doing in my bed?"

"Oh, well, they had some details to iron out and I'm still suffering from jetlag."

"Get out of my bedroom!"

"Just let me use the bathroom and freshen up a bit."

"Not in my bathroom or in my bedroom. Out! There's a sheriff's detective waiting for you to explain those men you brought into my home."

"Oh, uh, no, I don't want to talk to the sheriff."

Tough, Donald, I thought. I went back to the entry. "Alex, my cowardly brother-in-law is hiding out in our bedroom. I want him out of there, and he needs to explain those men to Detective Moreno."

Alex grinned. "A pleasure, lass." He headed for our bedroom and returned a few minutes later with Donald in tow. "Detective Moreno, this seems to be the actual host of the meeting here. He was apparently taking a nap while they carried on without him. Mr. Roth, perhaps you'd like to give us some background on your friends."

"Uh, Lawrence and Dwayne...I don't exactly know their last names."

"Mr. Roth, do you mean to tell me that you brought these men – whose full names you don't even know – into our home, and then allowed one of them to put his hands on my wife?"

"Um, I didn't see that happen."

"Beside the point; you were the supposed host here. That makes you responsible for the behavior of your guests and for the safety of your family members."

"Well, I have to hold at least one more meeting with them after I've been in contact with another of the principals in our business. After that they'll go back to Washington."

"Hold whatever meetings you want, but not in our house," I told him.

"Jennifer, this is extremely important to people at the national level and they think I have property here."

Alex stepped back into the conversation. "We know a nice real estate agent who might be able to help you out in a hurry, but I think you're missing our entire point. One of those men laid hands on my wife, and while I know she's very capable of defending herself, I don't expect her to have to defend herself against two large men with no help from her sister's husband."

"I never saw anything like that."

"Then you were looking the other way. If you aren't ready to defend the members of your own family, how can we expect you to uphold your oath of office to defend the country?"

"That's an insult! You can't talk to a congressman like that, and this isn't your country anyway. You should be deported. Arrested and deported."

"No sir, you don't have any authority to make that happen," Gabriel told him. "Your people were trespassing here and the homeowners had to call me to remove them and take back control of their own home. I hope you aren't threatening them; if so, I might have to arrest you."

Well, that got Donald's attention. "Jennifer, you can't let that happen. Tell him it was all a misunderstanding."

"Donald, you just threatened to have Alex arrested and deported for trying to protect his wife and property when your goons forced their way into our house and started pushing me around. Give me one good reason why we shouldn't ask Detective Moreno to arrest you."

"Well, it's not his house; it's your house so he has no standing here at all."

"Sorry, Donald, I told you that both of our names are on the title, but that's beside the point; I can also press charges unless we have your assurance that you will never try to bring those goons, or anyone else not properly introduced and approved by us to our home."

"You obviously need a guardian if you were stupid enough to put that fortune hunter's name on your assets! Your mother is supposed to be your legal heir."

"Detective Moreno, please escort this person off of our property; if he ever trespasses here again we will press charges."

"No, no, you can't do that. I need this place to meet with my congressional backers. We have important work to do."

Alex finally lost patience, "Detective Moreno, I think we've heard more than enough, get him out of here, and then come back for our full statement."

Alex winked and Gabriel was trying to stifle a grin, "Yes, sir." And he walked Donald out to his rental car and waited until he had cleared the driveway and turned right on the road.

When he got back to the house Alex had opened three bottles of beer. "Thanks, Gabe, from the looks of that pair, I wouldn't have wanted Jennifer to have to fend them off on her own."

I got the dogs out of the motor home and put them in the yard and then we all sat down in the living room section of our Great Room. My dining table was littered with two empty bottles of wine and dirty glasses and I could see red wine rings on my velvet table runner.

"Cheers, Superintendent MacLeod." Gabriel raised his beer bottle, "You called that correctly."

Alex raised his in return. "Thanks for stopping by, I might have had trouble trying to chuck them out on my own."

"Well, if you'd run into any difficulty and had to call 911, they might really have been arrested."

"If I had been here on my own," I told them, "that's exactly what would have happened. I'm still not sure that we shouldn't have done just that. The under-goon was making crude comments that seemed to imply that he had Donald's permission to 'enjoy my hospitality' whether or not I agreed."

"Do you know what their high-level meeting was about that they couldn't even discuss with you in the house?" Gabe asked.

"No, I only caught that one comment as I was being hustled out of my own home: The gorilla in charge said, 'Donny, boy, we don't care what it takes, you get that so-called expert in the Fish and Game to change his story and get our permit issued. You hear me?' It didn't make any sense to me."

"Hmm, I can't say that it does for me either, but you shouldn't have to worry about them again." He finished his beer. "So have a pleasant stay here this time; if you're going to the Fairgrounds for the dog show, at least the bicycles are a week later this year."

"Thank God," Alex and I said in unison.

I started to clear the empty bottles and wine glasses from the dining table but Alex stopped me. "Wait just a moment, lass, I'll just fetch my fingerprint kit and take the prints from those; we've both seen how useful randomly obtained fingerprints have proved in the past."

He asked me where each had been sitting. "Senior goon took the head of the table and Donald was sitting to his left. I never saw the muscle guy sit but his breath smelled of alcohol when we came in."

"He probably drank right out of the bottle. Well, I'll label the prints from these two wine glasses Roth and senior goon and just tuck them away in case we have further use for them."

There was a new chicken recipe I'd been dying to try. It called for chicken breasts, mandarin oranges, orange marmalade, chicken bouillon and Grand Marnier. I checked the ingredients before I started cooking. "That's funny, I was sure I had a full bottle of Grand Marnier but it's not here. This calls for a change of plans."

Before we went to bed ourselves I stripped our bed, changed the linens and dumped them into the washing machine. I didn't want to sleep on anything Donald or his goons might have touched. I went into our master bath for the towels and found the toilet seat up and one of my good, gold-bordered cocktail glasses balanced on the edge of the commode. "Alex, here's your last glass for fingerprints. It looks like muscle guy helped himself to my better glassware."

After breakfast Wednesday morning Alex took the Armada downtown for his deposition with the County Attorney, and I went shopping for our meals for a couple of weeks here.
By the time we both got back to the house, Alex was brimming over with a new project. "Hop in, lass, we're going to the home improvement store."
As he picked out plywood boards, gave cutting instructions, and then gathered up a collection of hardware, I finally figured out what he was doing. "You're making a whelping box!"
"Aye; just in case Misty decides to surprise us, but there's sure to come a time when we need a whelping box here. We'll put it together while we're here and decide how to paint it later."
My whelping box back home in San Diego was painted to look like a castle. Alex's up in Alberta was designed to look like a Tombstone saloon or bordello. It would be a challenge to figure out how to decorate this one, but I was sure my husband would come up with something creative.

We invited our neighbors, Augustin and Dominique for dinner, and local issues were the topic around our table.
"Alexander, there is a battle going on to build a gigantic subdivision in the desert east of here. That little town cannot support the huge numbers they propose to move in there. There are no hospitals or medical clinics. To say nothing of restaurants, or grocery stores; there are no basic services for the many thousands of people they plan to bring there. But most important, there is not enough water; there is a strong danger they will dry up the San Pedro River, and what that will do to our famous caverns is anyone's guess. Have you and Jennifer been to the Kartchner Caverns?"
"We have, but not for a couple of years."
"You should go again; it is such a treasure, and to think they

could possibly destroy it. Do you know the story? A living cave that was protected first by the young men who discovered it, next by the owners of the property, and finally by the State. They still take extreme precautions; when you enter there is an airlock so the outside air does not come in. The number of visitors is limited and they are strictly forbidden to touch the formations."

"We have a couple of free days before the shows," Alex pointed out. "Shall we go?"

"I'll call in the morning and see if it's possible to get a tour reservation."

"And if you go, drive through Benson and picture thousands and thousands of new houses springing up like *champignons*."

In the morning, yes, there was a tour available Thursday, the first one of the day at nine o'clock in the morning. I gave a credit card number to reserve it and then we had to figure out how to manage it. "It's at least an hour's drive, assuming no traffic delays."

"Is there a campground nearby? We do have the little motor home so we can just pack up the dogs and spend a night there."

"There's a campground right there, let me call again." Yes, there were sites available and I gave the credit card number again.

"Then we'll go out there this afternoon, and take a slow side trip to Benson to see what Augie is talking about."

"You're right; I've been through Benson, but never slowed down enough to see what's there."

CHAPTER FIVE
(*Thursday, November 7*)

While I was making breakfast, Alex busied himself on the computer. "Jennifer, the town of Benson has less than five thousand residents in only two thousand households. There appear to be about two dozen restaurants, mostly small, family places. We should have an excellent opportunity to form our own opinion about what Augie was telling us."

We got to the park late in the morning, plugged in, hooked up the water, walked the dogs, and then drove into Benson for lunch. We picked a family-style restaurant and were seated at a booth with menus at the table. I ordered an open-faced hot turkey sandwich with mashed potatoes, vegetables (canned) and a small sliver of cranberry jelly. Alex ordered the hot roast beef sandwich, and as the golden-aged waitress took our order Alex asked, "We've been hearing about the huge development planned for out here; what do you know about it?"

Well, that was an earful! "They're crazy! They're effing nuts. We can't handle so many people. Yeah, it would mean a lot more business for us, but there aren't enough restaurants in the whole town of Benson to feed all those people if they all went out to eat the same day. And we only have the one little hospital; what if a whole bunch of people get sick all at the same time?"

A voice from behind the counter called out, "Hey, Wanda, get a move on!"

She pulled out her pad again. "Did I get all of this correctly?" And then, *sotto voce*, "We're not supposed to have opinions here 'cause there've been some high-powered people in town taking measurements and talking up what that's going to do for our little economy. One of our regulars is a supervisor in Game and Wildlife and he blocked their permit for something or other, and then all hell broke loose. Yeah, Gene, one of them changed their mind about the side order, keep your cool." She lowered her voice again, "I overheard a couple of guys in here last week talking about taking a congressman out here to tour the proposed site so he could do some promotion."

"Waandaaaa!"

"Yeah, yeah, I'm coming."

"Well, that was interesting," I said after she was on her way back to the kitchen. "A congressman; just when we had one as an unwelcome guest."

"Aye, a congressman; that just might explain what your brother-in-law is doing out here, and why their discussions were so very secret."

"Well, I agree with Wanda, and Augie; that development doesn't sound like a good idea."

"And having the congressman back at our house with his crude friends sounds like an even worse idea."

I grinned, "No matter what pressure my mother brings to bear."

Our lunches were both delicious, even with the canned vegetables. "This is really good, Wanda, especially the carrots."

"Gene's a pretty good cook, even if we don't agree on politics."

After she dropped off the check, "Leave her a good tip, Alex."

"Oh, aye, her viewpoint was even better than the meal."

We spent the afternoon touring the grounds; the hummingbird garden, and the spectacular Visitor's Center. I almost wished to be a kid again as we watched a few youngsters crawling through some almost-real formations, and then we cruised the computer displays of the cavern attractions. I was drawn to the gift shop, and found a selection of southwest cookbooks. I thumbed through a couple of them and took one to the cash register. "Alex, I think I've found some new recipes to tempt you."

"Umm, I approve," he looked over the bookshelf himself and pulled out another book, "And how about this one?"

"I already have that one, and you've eaten well from it."

After a quick breakfast and dog walk we assembled at the check-in area, the tour guide gave us the rules for our tour: no cameras or cell phones, no pictures, no touching, no straying from the designated path. We got on a shuttle for the short ride up to the cave entrance and then entered an airlock. The temperature and humidity were carefully monitored and protected; this was a 'living' cave with water still helping the formations to continue growing. The scenery inside the cave was spectacular; we were awestruck all over again.

At one viewing overlook in the Big Room we found ourselves close enough to the park ranger to ask a question. "We've been hearing about a large development planned for the Benson area. Will that have an effect on the caverns?"

"We don't know that yet; experts are still evaluating the possibilities." She lowered her voice, "We're not supposed to have opinions on hot political topics, but of course we're concerned. The area really can't support that many more people; the town is too small and doesn't have the services, and there just isn't enough water. Just think of some seventy thousand more people flushing their toilets, doing laundry, washing dishes. The husband of one of our volunteers is a Fish and Wildlife supervisor. He denied a key permit because of concerns about the water, but there are very wealthy and important people who want this to happen, and in the current political climate, people who stand in the way are often just swept out of the way." She looked around at the rest of the tour group. They were mostly absorbed in the splendor all around us, but a few were starting to look to the tour guide for our next move.

"Thank you so much," Alex raised his voice, "this is truly magnificent, I'm glad we came."

We left through another airlock and rode the shuttle back down to the visitor center. As we walked back to the campground Alex said, "That was certainly informative."

"It certainly was. Between Wanda at the diner, and the park ranger here, people who have roots in this community generally seem to be opposed to the idea."

"Well, we're already agreed that your craven brother-in-law won't hold any more meetings with his goons at our house. I don't think there's anything else we can do to derail his project. Let's see what your new cookbook has to tempt us."

I skimmed the pages as Alex drove us back home. "I've found several possibilities to keep you entranced."

"My Scheherazade."

"Do you know, that simile occurred to me when I took over the Investigation Unit and had to keep them amused with new stories every week? I haven't lost my head yet there."

"And you certainly won't here; I expect to enjoy your cooking for many, many more years."

"Well, I think I have all of the ingredients on hand for at least one of them."

It took a bit over an hour to get back to our Tucson house and it was a shock to find a small rental sedan blocking access to our covered parking. "Alex, call Gabriel, if there's a car here, there must be someone who drove it here. I don't like this."

Detective Moreno arrived only a few minutes later. "Gabe, we don't know where the owner of this vehicle might be, but we thought we'd like to have you here to help find him."

"Happy to help, are we looking for any of the previous suspects?"

"It wouldn't be a surprise." I said, "Let's check all the entrances."

Luckily, all outside doors had been locked, so our unwelcome visitor was relaxed on a chair on the deck outside of our master bedroom, asleep, apparently.

Gabe took the lead. "Excuse me; why are you here?"

"What? None of your business; I'm waiting for my sister-in-law to come home."

"Sir, you were asked to leave here last week. Why are you here again?"

"My congressional backers are supposed to pick me up here for a trip out into the hinterlands." He turned to me. "Where have you been? I've been waiting here for almost an hour."

"Donald, you were told not to involve us, or come back to our house again. What in the hell are you thinking to come back here?"

"Well, they have to think this is my house, so you have to let me meet them inside the house in," he checked his watch, "less than ten minutes, so open the door, and then go get out of sight."

Alex stepped up onto the deck. "You seem to be missing our point. This is *not* your house, and after you allowed your very important friends to push around your wife's sister, we're no longer willing to participate in your charade."

"These aren't the same people. These men are far more important." He checked his watch again. "So open the door; they'll be here any minute."

"Gabe, we don't seem to be getting through to my brother-in-law. Would you escort him to his car and see that he leaves?"

"With pleasure. Come with me sir." He took Donald by the arm.

Donald shook him off, "This is official business; I'm a congressman, you can't force me to leave."

"Gabe, he may have won an election, but he won't be seated until January; he's actually not a congressman yet."

"Sir, I'm afraid I can ask you to leave, and in handcuffs if necessary. You wouldn't want your important friends to witness that, would you?"

That apparently got through to him and he headed toward his little rental, but he called over his shoulder, "Your mother is going to hear about this!"

As Gabe escorted him to his car, another one pulled in. As a detective now, Gabe was in street clothes, so without a uniformed deputy looming over him, Donald decided to bluff it out. "Hi guys, I need you to meet me back at the Hilton. Since I'm going to be busy with congressional duties for the next several months, I've decided to rent this place out, and I just had to show up here today to hand over the keys." He pointed to my motorhome with California plates, "They just arrived from out-of-state, but I gave them a quick walk-through, so we can go now. Just follow me back to the Hilton so I can leave this rental." He got into his car before they could respond or ask any questions, backed it around and headed away down the driveway.

Gabe walked back to us with a grin, "He threatened to tell your mother? My Mom always said, 'Wait till your father gets home' so is your mother that dangerous?"

"Gabe, I think my father may have died just to escape her. It's too early to offer you a beer, but come back later when you're off duty."

He smiled, "Thanks, but I promised my wife a dinner out tonight."

Alex said, "My wife just bought a new cookbook, maybe we can tempt the two of you with one of her recipes before we have to leave."

"That's definitely a tempting offer; I'll consult with the boss."

As I studied the recipe I had picked out from the new book I mused to Alex, "I can't believe my asshole brother-in-law still thinks he's entitled to use our house and our hospitality."

"Use, or abuse?"

"Abuse for sure, we don't want him back here under any circumstances."

"If he shows up here again, we might consider a restraining order."

"I certainly hope it doesn't come to that, but it would serve him right, and if he has to be taken away in handcuffs, I'll laugh all the way as they take him away down our driveway."

The new recipe was delicious, and, hoping we'd seen the last of my brother-in-law and his very important people, we prepared for the dog shows ahead.

Before we went to bed I checked the freezer and took inventory of what we already had on hand. Thick filet mignon steaks, several salmon filets and a bag of chicken parts. My wine cooler had taken a hit from Donald's goons and they had even left the dirty glasses on the table with obvious red wine rings on the velvet table runner. "We're okay for a few more days, but we'll have to stop at Safeway again soon, and this will go to the dry cleaner around the corner."

CHAPTER SIX
(*Friday, November 8 – Monday, November 11*)

In order to give Monty an ongoing role in dog shows we had decided that his young grandson should be the one to uphold the family honor in Best of Breed competition while Monty was entered in the Utility obedience class. With parking a challenge at the Rillito Racetrack plus hours between Utility and breed judging, I had only entered him at the Friday and Monday shows, and then all four days the following weekend at the fairgrounds. I didn't understand why the show committee felt we should be punished for competing at the highest levels of training, but the Utility ring time was eight o'clock in the morning all four days. Breed judging was early afternoon, just after the judges' lunch break. I felt sorry for any exhibitors who came for both breed and obedience and had to sit around for all of the hours in between; at least I could go back to our house and relax until our next ring time.

"I'll cook breakfast, lass, and do you want me to go out there with you and cheer from a distance?"

"No, just toast an English muffin for now. And then you can start your pancakes cooking when I call to tell you I'm on my way back. Oh, and while you're waiting, you may as well put together the whelping box in half of the guest suite just in case Misty doesn't want to wait until we get back to San Diego."

I got to the ring and found a notice prominently posted at the entrance, "Mrs. Janet Webb will not judge obedience today. Any affected exhibitors may apply for a refund of their entry fees." Well, I didn't know Janet Webb, I didn't recognize the name of the substitute judge, and we had to qualify three times to earn the Utility Dog title, so I'd stay in the game, at least for now. If I didn't fill out the form for a refund before the start of judging, my entry was forfeit if I didn't compete. But I didn't think I'd run into another judge like the one I encountered at young Dragon's very first obedience trial. That judge looked like he was actually trying to fail the dogs. I decided to take my chances and watch what this judge did with the dogs before us. We were last in the ring since the regulations suggested that dogs that had the same jump height should compete in order before the stewards had to change the jumps.

Utility was the highest level of canine obedience, the PhD of this phase of the sport. Monty had already competed in Utility in Canada during the summer and had taken home the club trophy. Our breed was somewhat handicapped in obedience competition by the shape of our dogs; the 'corgi sit' was often slightly lopsided and could lose us a point every time a sit was required.

I was seated several feet back from ringside as the larger breeds competed ahead of us. A woman with a pretty sable German Shepherd was pacing back and forth in front of us, practicing turns and sits, and signals. Strictly illegal; the regulations stated that there was to be 'no intensive drilling' on the show grounds, and here she was doing just that right in front of me. "Excuse me; don't you know that isn't allowed?"

"Don't bother me; I'm getting ready to go in the ring."

When she left the ring, after non-qualifying in both Signal Exercise and Scent Discrimination, she stormed right over to where I was sitting and demanded, "What are you doing at this ring? Have you ever even done obedience? Don't you know better than to talk to someone before they go in the ring?"

"Yes; don't you? I'm next."

"Well, you probably won't qualify either!" And she jerked the leash and stalked off with her dog.

The order in which the exercises would be performed was posted at the ring entrance, and I was happy to see that we started with Scent Discrimination. It was an exercise that Monty loved, and would get him off to a good start, as opposed to the Signal Exercise which tended to make him sleepy.

This exercise was in two parts; the judge would choose one of three sets of scent articles and indicate the specific article I was to handle. After I put my scent on the article the judge would drop the entire set on the ground and tell me to send my dog. The three sets were: wood, leather and metal. After we did the exercise with the first article we repeated it with the second set. Today's articles were wood and then metal, and metal was something that dogs often weren't comfortable picking up. However, since Monty had earlier this year retrieved a gun that had been pointed at me only seconds before he brought it to me, I didn't doubt that he'd shine in this exercise.

The Directed Retrieve was next, where he had to retrieve the one specified glove of three located across the ring from us. This was another exercise that got Monty's blood moving so when it was followed by the Signal Exercise and the Moving Stand for Examination he was still fired up enough to give us a decent score. We ended with Directed Jumping where I would send my dog to the far end of the ring and then, at the judge's direction, indicate either the bar jump or the high jump. The exercise was then repeated for the other jump. It was a good exit line for Monty and we came away certain of a Utility leg. Our competitors were two Golden Retrievers, a Shetland Sheepdog, the German Shepherd and a Border Collie. I didn't expect High Score with a crooked-sit Corgi, but we ended up in fourth place when one of the Goldens almost did fall asleep during the Signal Exercise.

Monty's first American Utility leg was worth a photo and the steward paged our good friend and professional photographer, Robin St. Clair, to our ring. As we waited for Robin to set up the information on his official display I asked the judge what happened to the one he replaced. "Not that I'm complaining, I want you to know."

"I honestly don't know. You might ask the superintendent. I'm only provisional, Ned Emory grabbed me this morning and asked if I could fill in; I was actually entered in Open myself, but I obviously had to forego my own Open leg. Don't worry, yours counts, and that's a really nice working dog."

"Thanks. He's a Best in Show winner here, and in Canada, but I was advised by some top professionals that he should retire in favor of his grandson."

"What a grand dog, and how lucky that you can give him a second career." I didn't mention that my beloved Monty had failed at the third career – herding dog – but his grandson had possibly saved my life from a flock of stampeding sheep.

I called Alex with the good news and he promised to have the pancakes ready to serve when I pulled up at the house. He hugged me, and praised Monty, and the pancakes were fluffy and delicious. We had a nice rosette and a small, but pretty trophy featuring a high jump. A really high jump; the gold-toned trophy looked like the correct height for the German Shepherd that hadn't qualified. "We'll just let people believe you earned your leg over that jump," I told Monty as I put my plate down for him to lick.

When we left with Dragon for breed judging after an early lunch, Monty was snoozing on a rug in the living room section of our great room.

The entry was small today and Dragon was Best of Breed, and then won a Group third. A thrilling start to his career as a Special.

While we waited at Robin's photo setup I asked him if he had heard anything about our deceased obedience judge. "No, darling, but when I'm sitting around gossiping with Clair and Ned I'll ask."

Dragon was Best of Breed again Saturday and Sunday, but with higher entries over the weekend, no Group placements.

Monday morning we were back at the Utility ring again at eight o'clock. The order of exercises was different today, but again started with one that Monty liked: the Directed Retrieve. Once again the first exercise got his blood moving and he gave another stellar performance. One of the Border Collies got confused on her second scent article – they were metal and leather today. The German Shepherd hadn't even checked in, and Monty ended up in first place for his second UD leg, and a run-off for High Score in Trial. A Sheltie competing for the lower, CDX, title beat us by a point for High Score, but it would still be worth a picture.

Breed judging followed obedience closely enough that we had both come here with both dogs today. Dragon was pulled in the final six in Group, and after several agonizing minutes he made the final cut for a fourth place.

We took both dogs to Robin's photo setup and had the obedience judge paged.

I posed Monty on the platform with his Utility trophy, and first place rosette, Robin snapped the picture, Monty got down and Alex brought Dragon to the platform. Dragon hopped up more athletically than his grandsire had, and once again I had to recognize that my beloved dog was aging. Lucky indeed that we had a second career.

The obedience judge left and while we waited for our breed judge I asked Robin if he'd found out anything about our deceased judge.

"Clair didn't have much information; she said what she heard was that the judge and her husband died in a house fire."

Just a quiet dinner for the two of us tonight. I thawed a lovely salmon filet, skinned a couple of carrots, and got out my recipe for Bourbon-glazed carrots. The dogs were fed and Alex had opened a bottle of white wine. He put his arm around me, kissed the back of my neck – and the phone rang.

"*Merde*! Does this remind you of our Tucson National?"

"Maybe it's our Nigerian millions. Hello? Oh, Gabriel, you want Alex? Here he is." I handed the phone over.

"Oh? Aye, we're home. Now? Well, my lovely and patient wife always loves a mystery, so come on over and we'll hash this out."

"What?"

"Gabriel has a case that he'd like to consult on, and it seems to merge with some of the other things we've been hearing."

We first met Deputy – now Detective – Gabriel Moreno right here four years ago, in a storm that triggered a flash flood that ultimately carried off a killer who planned to make me his next victim. He had become a trusted friend who often had a beer with us while we consulted on the latest difficulty. Which, just last week, had been my problem brother-in-law.

The doorbell rang, Monty and Dragon ran to the door, barking. Misty ambled out from the half of the guest suite that had been set up as a potential whelping room.

"Detective Moreno, we're always happy to see you, especially when we don't have to ask you to remove someone from our home. I've just opened a bottle of wine, will you join us, or have a beer?"

"Beer, thanks, and I won't keep you long tonight, but I wanted to run this by you, and ask if, by any chance, you'd like to visit the site with me?"

I saw Alex's face light up. "I'd be delighted, and I'm honored you should ask; when?"

"Tomorrow, if you're free."

"Our dog shows are finished for a few days, we had nothing planned for tomorrow. Jennifer? What's your opinion?"

"Well, of course you should go; you shouldn't even have to ask," but we both remembered my late husband, Kent, who frequently chose his job over our marriage. "Tell us about your situation."

"You may have heard of the controversy out near Benson; the big development they want to put in that's bigger than most people think the area can support."

Alex and I looked at each other. "Aye, we've discussed it with our neighbor, we brought it up to a waitress and a park ranger out in Benson, and we heard quite an earful."

"What's more," I added, "the waitress at the diner in Benson mentioned some 'high-powered people' in town doing measurements, and overheard a conversation about a congressman going out there for information so he could promote it. When we just had a congressman you had to escort off our property, twice."

Gabriel looked up at that. I told him, "Remember what I told you I heard one of Donald's goons say? 'Donny boy, get that Fish and Wildlife guy to issue our permit,' or something like that."

"I remember. Do you think your brother-in-law is part of that scheme?"

"It's starting to sound like it."

"Is that a problem for you and Alex?"

"Not on your life. Or mine. Donald was part – I hope an unwitting part – of a scheme to kill either Alex, or me, so the family's spiritual advisor could take control of the assets left to me by my late husband. I no longer trust any member of my own family."

"Well, that Fish and Wildlife guy just happens to be my case."

"How so?" Alex asked.

"He's dead, and the circumstances are suspicious. He and his wife died last week in a home fire. They live on a large piece of property in an area of mini-ranches out near Benson..."

"I thought Benson was in Cochise County," I said. "How come the Pima County Sheriff is involved?"

"His house was about three-quarters of a mile inside our county line; almost ten miles to the west of Benson, so it's our case."

"What are the suspicious circumstances?"

"They're quite some distance from any neighbors, so by the time anyone spotted the blaze the home was fully engulfed. But here's the problem; they have several of the markers of a home security company around the property. There were stickers on the windows and a stake with the company logo at the entrance to the property. So I called the Mescal Fire District. They got a call from a neighbor who saw the fire from about a quarter-mile away; they never got an alarm from the home itself."

"Had they just stopped paying for the service?"

"No; I called the company; their contract was active and it

included an alarm system and smoke detectors. It should have transmitted an alarm to the fire district."

"You're right," Alex said. "Those are suspicious circumstances. I assume you've had the arson team out?"

"Yes, and the opinion was, no, it wasn't arson. Apparently someone cleaned out the hearth and then left a couple of cardboard boxes full of the ashes on either side of the patio door off the master bedroom. There were also a couple of stacks of vinyl siding leaning against the wall next to that door and when the hot ashes burned through the cardboard the fire ignited the siding and released toxic fumes into the bedroom. I talked to the fire district captain; he just shook his head and said it was obviously a case of really terminal stupidity. Actually, what he said was, 'Geez! They may as well just have poured kerosene on the house.' Which I took to mean it was really dumb on their part."

"So where do I come in?"

"I have a bad feeling about it. I would really appreciate it if you'd just come out to the house with me and see if you can spot anything we might have missed. We're at a loss as to who or why would someone want to murder Bryce Webb, or his wife, Janet."

"Janet? Janet Webb?" That got my attention. "Alex, that was the name of the obedience judge who was replaced Friday. Remember when Robin told us what he had learned from the superintendent?"

"Aye, and then the Ranger at the cavern told us that the wife of the Fish and Wildlife guy was a volunteer there."

"Gabe, let me go along tomorrow too. While you two examine the possible crime scene, I'll go into Benson and see if I can talk to Wanda at the diner again. I have this sinking feeling that my sister's husband was involved in possible pressure on that official to issue a vital permit for that huge development we've been hearing about."

"She's right," my husband said. "Even our homicide detective in San Diego has called her a valuable partner. If she learns anything she may give you another witness to interview. And while we're at it, Gabe, if you could pave the way for Jennifer to also meet with our ranger from the Kartchner Caverns tour; that could give us some insight from the wife's point of view."

"I can ask the Cochise Sheriff's department to contact her and make an appointment. I assume you remember her name?"

"Of course; R. Barber was on her nametag," Alex told him.

"What time do we have to leave tomorrow?" I asked.

"The scene is secured and not going anywhere; no storms forecasted. If we go there in time for Jennifer to have lunch with Wanda, and work around when your ranger might be available we can get a lot done. I'll call you with the times.   How early is too early?"

Alex looked at me, I shrugged. "I guess whenever you need to call us."

"It won't be too early; my wife would also object. By the time I make the phone calls, you should have as much time as you need for breakfast."

Gabe thanked us for the beer, and for the offer of help, and pulled out. "We still have time for your outstanding dinner," Alex said, "and then, Gabe promised not to call too early."

CHAPTER SEVEN
(*Tuesday, November 12*)

True to his word, it was almost nine in the morning when Gabe called. Alex answered and put the phone on speaker. "Alex, Jennifer, I've set up a meeting with the Kartchner Caverns ranger at eleven; Jennifer can meet with her there and then go into Benson for another lunch with Wanda. We should take two vehicles; can I pick you up soon?"

"Aye, we had breakfast some time ago, we're ready to go."

"I'll see you in about fifteen minutes." When he arrived he said Alex should go with him while I drove out to the caverns to meet with the ranger. "Do you want to tackle Wanda on your own, or would you like us to join you there for lunch? It's about an hour out there so we should get going."

"Let me try her on my own. If it looks promising you can join me there so we can leave her a bigger tip."

I drove the small motor home out to the caverns, went to the information desk in the Visitor's Center and told the ranger, "I'm here to interview Ranger Barber; it was arranged in advance."

"Oh, yes, we rearranged her schedule so she could meet with you. Do you need space for a camera crew?"

I wondered how creative Gabe and the Cochise County Sheriff had been. "No, this will just be a one-on-one interview. I have everything I need in a small motor home out in the parking lot. I'll have her join me there."

Our ranger met me at the desk and I invited her out to the motor home. When we were comfortable I opened the conversation. "Ranger Barber..."

"Just call me Ramona."

"Thanks, and I'm Jennifer. We were on your tour last week and my husband asked you about that huge development being planned out here."

"Oh, well I think I told him that we're supposed to keep our opinions to ourselves."

"I understand, but you mentioned the wife of the Fish and Wildlife supervisor was one of your volunteers."

"Yes, poor Jan, she was a lovely person; always happy and sunny, and she loved this park. They had lived here so long that they knew the family that owned the property, and they met the students – the amateur cavers – who made the discovery. She used to talk about those early days when the discovery was still a secret; how exciting it was to be in on the secret. She told us they even kidnapped the Governor, brought him out blindfolded, and took him underground to see it in an attempt to get the State to adopt it as a park. Of course, that could just be a legend after all these years."

Ramona looked like she would have been in about Sixth Grade when the park was finally opened to the public two decades ago.

"Yes, I've read some of those stories and they're fascinating. The actual reason I'm here is that my husband is a well-known forensics expert, and a friend of ours is a Pima County Detective who asked him to investigate the possible homicide of Janet and her husband."

"Homicide? You mean someone killed her?"

"It's possible that the house fire wasn't an accident. And her husband was the one who denied a key permit for that development."

"Are you serious? Someone actually killed them?"

"Yes, maybe; our friend, the deputy, is suspicious. He and my husband are looking at the scene this morning, and I volunteered to meet with you and ask if there was anything you could contribute to a possible investigation."

"Nothing in the way of evidence; Jan wasn't a gossip, but she sometimes shared her frustration when we were on breaks. She told us recently that her husband was getting pressure from a higher-up in Washington who wanted him to reverse his decision on the permit he'd denied. Now, this is only what she mentioned to us over coffee, but apparently there was an invitation for an important official to spend a weekend at a lodge in Idaho, with some controlled trophy hunting, and then someone contacted her husband and strongly suggested that his career was at stake if he didn't change his opinion. She was as low as I've ever seen her. 'He may have to just retire rather than do that,' she said, and they weren't really ready to do that. He loved his job as much as she loved volunteering here at the Caverns."

"Did she ever mention anyone by name?"

"If she did I either didn't recognize the name, or just wasn't paying attention. Wait a minute, there was that time just last week...." She paused to collect her thoughts. "No name, but she was clearly angry. She'd been leading a group in the hummingbird garden, and when she came in for lunch she was, well, really pissed off is the only way to describe it. She said she answered a call the night before from someone who asked for her husband and said he was a congressman."

"But she didn't say who it was?"

"No, but she said she heard him tell the caller, 'No, goddammit, you can't come to my house for a face-to-face meeting! There's nothing more you can say without insulting my integrity more than you already have.' She said he slammed down the phone. And then he told her, 'That son of a bitch told me that the favor and goodwill of a congressman can do a lot to advance my career.' She said her husband was so furious when he got off the call that she was actually worried about his blood pressure.

The hair on the back of my neck prickled, much like Monty or Dragon's reaction to a threat. That phrase was only too familiar. I asked a few more questions, but I had apparently drained Ramona of everything she could remember. "Thank you so much, I think you've been more help than you realized. If what you've told me is as valuable as I believe, would you be willing to give an official interview?"

"Of course; Jan was part of our team. We all miss her."

Next was another lunch at Wanda's diner.

"Well, hi there, you're a new face who's been here before. Are you here for our lovely winter season?"

"Actually, Wanda, I'm here to pick your brain to help with an investigation. My husband was with me here last week, and today he's assisting a Pima County Detective. Do you remember when we asked you about that huge development and you said something about a congressman?"

"Yeah, and I got chewed out by the boss for taking so long at your table."

"I won't waste your time today while you're working, but can we meet you privately later?"

"Sure, we're only open for breakfast and lunch, and by three o'clock we've cleaned up and gone home. Here's my number." She wrote it on my napkin.

"Waaandaa! C'mon and step it up, quit your gossiping!"

"Oh, shut up, Gus! She's a snowbird and she's asking for directions."

I ordered another hot turkey, open-face, sandwich, and while I was waiting I phoned Alex. "Lots of information for you, When I leave Wanda's, can I order to-go for you and Gabe?"

"Aye, and then join us here," and he read off an address. "Put it into the GPS in the motor home, but call again if she takes you down some unknown road."

I chuckled, remembering the time he told me of a GPS unit that tried to route him down a dirt pole-line road when he was towing a trailer. This GPS was a lot friendlier than Alex's old one; the address was a little less than ten miles west of Benson and there were no locked gates on my route. The Webb's home was on a large property of possibly ten acres or more; it was hard to guess without fences along the property lines, but I could barely see the next closest house. There were corrals – empty now – and a Barnmaster modular home for horses. And, the ruin of what had been their house.

"Ahh, thank you, lass," as I handed out their sandwiches. "I'm so grateful to our friend Gabe for inviting me out here." But he wasn't smiling. "After a wee bit of snooping, this was almost certainly arson." He turned to Gabe. "No criticism of your local investigators; they had no idea there was a political agenda going on. But once we took a closer look, all of the batteries in every smoke detector, or other security device were put in improperly. A couple of them were missing altogether. Now, we all see occasional negligence or carelessness, as in failure to replace the batteries, but every single one put in wrong? Backwards, or not making contact? This in the home of a high level government scientist? It doesn't make any sense."

"Could it just be a really weird coincidence?" Gabe asked around a mouthful of sandwich.

"Coincidences like this make my skin itch. Gabe, can you contact the medical examiner? And then get us the autopsy results?"

"Of course; what should we be looking for?"

"If the entire alarm system was intentionally disabled by person or persons unknown, I would want to look at the fingerprints on every battery in those disabled alarms. There should only be the prints of one of the homeowners on those batteries, most likely his, just given the normal height difference between men and women. Any other fingerprints should be suspicious. And then," he turned to me, "remember the Hoffners?"

"Oh yes; their spiked wine bottle."

"Aye." He told Gabe the story. "This sweet old couple was somehow seen as a threat to a crooked sheriff's deputy over in California. He and his partner in crime drugged their opened bottle of wine, and plugged the furnace vent to try to kill them with carbon monoxide poisoning. I would look for anything that might have sedated them so they wouldn't wake up if one of them smelled the smoke, or heard the fire district truck."

Gabe finished his sandwich. "That vinyl siding; the toxic fumes might have left them unable to respond."

"That would have been a bit of a gamble; I'd still look for something that might have drugged them."

"So, do you agree that this may have been a homicide?"

"Oh, aye; Gabe, lad, you've done a magnificent job of following your suspicions and coming up with a case. Jennifer, on the surface it was as simple as the homeowner cleaning out the hearth and then dumping the ashes in a cardboard box too near the door. A few live embers in the box to reignite the flames was all it took."

"Why did they put the ashes from the hearth outside the bedroom door?"

"It was one of those see-through fireplaces between the living room and the bedroom."

"Okay, I guess that makes sense."

"Except that their hearth was still so full of ash that they couldn't have possibly cleaned it that day or the day before. And, in spite of the fire in the house, the ashes in the fireplace were cold, while the fire apparently started in a box of hot ash next to the patio doors from their bedroom. Gabe, in my opinion, you have a homicide here, and my lovely and talented wife can now probably give you some suspects to investigate."

"Huh? How?"

"Jennifer, your story."

"I talked with our ranger this morning; she didn't have much direct information, but she repeated the last conversation she remembered from Janet Webb. She told me Janet was really pissed off when she went to lunch that day. She told her coworkers that her husband had a call from someone who said he was a congressman, and when he got off the call that she was actually worried about his blood pressure. He slammed the phone down, she said. Ranger Ramona quoted a phrase that I've, unfortunately, heard before."

"What's that?"

"The goodwill and favor of a congressman can do a lot for your career."

Gabe's face showed sudden comprehension. "You mean your brother-in-law? The one we had to remove from your house twice?"

"Remember that strange scrap of conversation I overheard when Donald's goons were in the house? When the chief goon told Donald to get the objection to that permit reversed?"

"Oh; yes, yes, I do. You think your brother-in-law and his associates are connected to this homicide?"

"Gabe, it hurts to have to say this about someone connected to my family, but yes; Donald was willing to write off their spiritual advisor's attempt to kill me as simply evidence that I overdramatized everything. I hope Donald isn't stupid enough to have gone along with a homicide, but where his own self-interest is concerned, he tends to turn a blind eye to the consequences for anyone else."

"Well, I'm so glad you thought to call me when those two goons were pushing you around in your own home. I still have their identifying information, as well as your brother-in-law's. They're all out-of-state, and we sure don't have any evidence to charge anyone and ask for extradition, but it's a start. Superintendent MacLeod, I'm the first to admit that I'm fairly new as a detective, and I'm a little out of my depth when it comes to investigating high-level politicians, and out-of-state suspects. I'm open to advice from an expert."

Alex turned to me. "Jennifer, your contacts today may give us the best next step."

"We should call Wanda when she's off work and talk to her, and then, Gabe, do you have a police artist?"

"The Sheriff's Department has an artist, yes."

"Could I sit down with the artist and get portraits made of Donald's goons, and then show those portraits to Wanda?"

"If I can make it happen, I will. What about your brother-in-law?"

"Aha! I can do better than an artist's drawing. We made a good friend back in his home state, the District Attorney. Forrest Willoughby will be able to get us a recent campaign photo of Donald so I don't have to dig out their wedding photo and have your artist age it. Let's go talk to Wanda and see how much she can tell us, and if she'll be willing to try to identify her customers from your artist's renderings."

Gabe was scrolling through his phone. "Hang on a minute. When we chucked those guys out of your house the first time I just snapped their driver's licenses with my phone rather than write it all down. We already have their pictures."

"I don't know; I hope I don't look like my driver's license photo."

"Have a look. If necessary we can have you work with the artist to make them look more human."

I looked, and passed the phone to Alex. "Aye, I see your point, lass, these pictures were taken too close-up and the faces are a bit distorted. But between these and Gabe's artist, you can put together some recognizable faces. Are these even worth showing to Wanda?"

"I don't think so. Let's talk to Wanda and see how cooperative she wants to be, and then, if she's going to be a real help, we'll enlist her."

"Mrs. MacLeod, you'd make a good partner!"

"She's heard that before, Gabe, from our own homicide detective back in San Diego."

"And, as I've had to remind him, you can't afford me. On the other hand, I'm happy to volunteer."

"And I'm happy to have all the help I can get. When are we supposed to talk to Wanda?"

"She said she was off at three. That's another twenty minutes and I don't think we want to call her before then; her boss was already annoyed that she was spending so long at my table."

We were about fifteen minutes away from Benson so we drove back into town, waited another few minutes, and then I poked in the number Wanda had given me.

"Yeah, who's this?"

"Wanda, I'm Jennifer, I had lunch there today and took a to-go order for my husband and a Sheriff's deputy. You said you could talk to me after you were off work."

"Oh, yeah, how do you want to do it?"

"We're still in town and if we could meet with you, in private, my husband and our friend, a Sheriff's deputy, would like to run a few questions by you."

"What, am I a suspect or something?"

"No, but you may know something that can help us arrest one."

"Well, sure, that sounds more interesting than slinging plates all day." She gave me directions to her house; a single-wide, pre-fab in a small subdivision of similar homes.

There was a small, old sedan parked in the driveway. "It looks like she's home," I told Alex, "I saw that old car parked off to the side of the restaurant."

Gabe pulled up behind us. "Do you want to go smooth the way for us?"

"No, she's expecting all three of us."

As I rang the doorbell, Alex stood with his back to the house, looking out across the street. Wanda opened the door. "Well, come on inside all of you. I dunno what I'm going to tell the neighbors about all these strangers coming to my house."

Alex said, "Aye, I saw at least one curtain twitch while we were waiting. Try this story: Detective Gabriel Moreno of the Pima County Sheriff's Department is the nephew of your sister-in-law, while Jennifer and I are his aunt and uncle on the other side of the family. He brought us here for a tour of your marvelous Caverns."

Wanda laughed. Actually, she sort of cackled. "That works for me. Hang on a minute while I get my shopping list and write down all your names; my memory isn't good enough to remember all of your names. Or how you're supposedly related to me."

Alex took her small pad and wrote down our names and fictional relationships. "If anyone comes to ask you about our visit, swallow this paper."

"Do what? Are you kidding me?"

"Wanda, my husband can often be outrageous, especially if you happen to have a mouthful of Scotch, but there's a nugget of truth in what he said. Did you know Bryce or Janet Webb?"

"Oh, yeah, the Fish and Wildlife guy. His wife worked out at the Caverns. They were regulars, came in for breakfast about once a week. I really liked them, and he was against that big development they've been talking about out here for months."

"You said something the first time we were at your restaurant about a conversation you overheard involving a congressman, or someone talking about a congressman. Do you remember that conversation?"

"Sorta, mostly because they stuck out like a turd in a punchbowl. There were three of them; two in suits when most of our customers are in jeans and cowboy shirts. Like you folks."

True, we had dressed casually today to blend in with the local population, and the other diners at lunch time had been just as casual.

"The third one, the one I guessed had something to do with the development had on Western clothes like he was playing dress up. His boots were so new they squeaked, he had a big, shiny belt buckle like a rodeo rider when I'm sure he never got nearer than a Western movie, and you could see the creases in his shirt, like it just came off the shelf. And they were pushy and rude. Like, we're supposed to go back to the table after the food is served and ask if everything is okay, and do they need anything else. So this one big guy who looks like a bouncer says, 'Get outta here, Granny, if we need anything we'll holler for it.' I had to stop myself from telling him off, and then I shoulda, because they didn't even leave a tip."

"What did you do?"

"I cleaned the tables behind them and on both sides, and I listened. The bouncer didn't seem to have any function except to tote the boss's briefcase and keep people away from their table. Another couple'a townies came in and sat down at one of the tables I'd just cleaned, and the bouncer told them to 'go sit somewhere else; that table's reserved.' Anyway, you want to know what they talked about. I got the impression that the cowboy was either the developer, or someone who worked for him. He talked about surveying and easements and greenspace, but he told the guy with the briefcase that he had to get 'that enviro-nazi' to issue the effing permit, and briefcase guy told him that's what the tame congressman was for, so don't worry, we're on it. And that's all I really remember. I tried to think if there was anything else while I finished up this afternoon, but I really think that's all."

"Wanda, we think some of those guys showed up at a home in Tucson where Detective Moreno had to be called to get rid of them. He took pictures of their driver's licenses. You know how awful driver's license photos can be. Would you be willing to take a look and see if they look anything like the men at that table?"

"Sure."

Gabe got out his phone, scrolled through it for a couple of minutes and then held it out to Wanda.

"Oh, jeeze, I see what you mean. Yeah, I think those were the guys, but I can't be a hundred percent sure."

"What about the congressman? Was there ever anyone here that was identified as someone from Congress?"

"Not that I could tell. He was apparently their ace in the hole, or up the sleeve."

"Well, Gabe can get us access to a Sheriff's artist who might be able to make those driver's license photos look more human. There are a couple of other people who have seen them. If we can get decent portraits, may we bring them back out for you to look at?"

"Sure, but maybe call me at home after three so my boss doesn't get all bent out of shape again. I mean, you guys are always welcome at the diner, but Gus is kind of nosy, and if you're doing an investigation, he's going to be all over that. Come to think of it, if you're doing an investigation, do you think those guys had something to do with Bryce and Jan dying?"

Gabe answered, "There seems to be a connection that we're looking into, but I don't want to tell you so much that you act like you're suspicious if they come back to your diner."

"Nah, don't worry about that. If they come back they're sure to be rude enough to piss me off again. But if they do, I'll try to give the closest tables a super cleaning."

"Wanda, lassie, we've enjoyed your outstanding food and exceptional service; don't put yourself at risk, leave that to us."

"I think it's been fifty years since anyone called me a lassie. That was almost as good as your tip. Don't worry; I've been around a lot longer than those punks."

She had served us glasses of homemade iced tea. "In summer we make sun tea. For you snowbirds, that's when we don't even have to boil the water, just set out the pitcher with the tea bags in it."

"Wanda, we actually have a house here so we know summers."

"Well, come back in summer and I'll make sun tea for you."

We said goodbye to her at the front door, but before we could get away she grabbed Gabe and gave him a hug. "Just in case the neighbors are still watching. But if someone killed Bryce and Jan, you be sure you get the SOB."

"Yes, ma'am." He grinned, and turned around and waved at her before getting into his own small pickup truck.

Alex and I went on back home. "Jennifer, lass, I noticed that you didn't identify us as the others who had contact with Donald's goons."

"I thought it might be helpful to just keep a few aces up our own sleeves."

"Ah, clever idea."

"Well, I really didn't want Wanda to know so much that she could become a threat to them. I think we're already pretty sure they're willing to commit murder."

"Gabe will get back to us with an appointment to meet with their artist, and then we'll go back out with better pictures."

"He said their driver's licenses were from Washington, DC so Forrest Willoughby can't help us with them."

"He may have contacts there."

"But we won't have any contacts even when Donald arrives there."

"There could come a time when you drop his name – without letting him know, naturally."

I laughed at that. "And here we are home."

"With another alien vehicle in the driveway."

But it was Gabe's small pickup, and he knew better than to block our access to the covered parking area. "I won't keep you, but knowing that you have weekend plans, I was able to arrange a meeting with the artist tomorrow. Nine-thirty if that works."

Alex and I looked at each other. "Yes," we said in unison.

"You know where the local sub-station is, right?"

"Aye, we'll be there."

CHAPTER EIGHT
(*Wednesday, November 13*)

We met Gabe mid-morning at the local sheriff's substation and he took us to a small conference room and introduced the artist. "All three of us have seen these two men, and I photographed their driver's licenses, so how would you like to proceed?"

"Are we doing this for court?"

"No, we just want the best possible picture to show another potential witness."

"Okay; if you were going to court with this I'd want each of you to work with me separately and then see how closely you agree. But let's do it as a group and then, see if you all agree."

"Mrs. MacLeod spent the most time in their presence, Superintendent MacLeod and I arrived on the scene later to remove them from her home."

The artist looked at the driver's license photos and then asked Gabe to print them as close to life size as he could without distortion. "If they get too pixelated I won't have a good image to work with." When Gabe brought back the printouts – about four times the size of the license – the artist asked me to go first. "Here's the first one, Dwayne Maguirk. How do you picture him compared to this photo?"

"First, he's grinning for his license photo – who does that? He never smiled when he was trying to push me around in my own home, and I'll bet he never smiled when our other witness saw him."

She took me through Maguirk's features: nose, ears and lips each in turn and when I finally said, "That's close enough to him that you could issue a 'Wanted' poster," she smiled, and asked Alex and then Gabe to look at it and add their comments. Both of them thought I had pictured him slightly larger in body mass – she had added a torso complete with shirt, tie and jacket. "Dark suit or light?" It was a pencil drawing without color. After I was satisfied, and Gabe and Alex had both viewed the drawing, the artist told me, "Here's where we get different witness statements; you're a petite female, and you viewed the subject as larger and more threatening than your tall husband or our homicide detective. But you all agree that this is the face of your possible suspect. How about the next one?"

Once again I went first, but my interaction with Lawrence DeLuca was much more limited than with his goon. Interestingly, because I hadn't actually felt as much of a threat from him, our assessments of the artist's rendering were almost identical. The artist passed around the second portrait and we all agreed that we could take those portraits to our other witness for her opinion.

The artist scanned and printed the portraits for us. When we got back to the house I called Muriel Willoughby, the wife of the Fulton County District Attorney.

"Jennifer MacLeod, how lovely to hear from you again. Are you all planning to visit our city again?"

"Not in the near future, but my brother-in-law, your new congressman, seems to be involved in something unsavory again."

"Oh, no, how embarrassing for you."

"It's worse than that; there may have been a homicide here..."

"In San Diego? Are you working with Damaris Colton on it?"

"No, we're not in San Diego right now; we're at our house in Tucson."

"Your summer home?" Muriel asked, and I could hear the lurking chuckle.

"Oh, God no! We're here now for the dog shows. We also both gave depositions in a very sad case of child abuse. We'll have to tell you about that later."

"We would be so pleased to have you do that over cocktails, but let me call Forrest to hear about your current problem. He's out pruning back the roses, or watching Sal pruning the roses."

Forrest came on the line a few minutes later. "Alex and Jennifer, it's good to hear from you again. I had a very successful quail season with your little motor home, and we have enough in the freezer to thaw some for you. Hallie has a recipe she won't even share with us. We would love to invite you for supper again."

Forrest had been captivated by our original Mercedes motor home at just about the time that Alex was talking me into one just a little bit bigger — and with a full-sized fridge. The trade worked out beautifully for all of us. "So tell me about your current problem."

"I'll try to make this as concise as I can." I said. "There's a small town near Tucson, population about five thousand, with a single twenty-two bed hospital. A major developer is trying to build a humungous housing development there; it could add as many as seventy thousand to the local population. Most of the people we've talked to are opposed to the whole idea – with good reason, we believe."

"Oh my, yes, we heard about that, it must have been some weeks ago, on a national news show," Muriel said.

"Well, a Fish and Wildlife official turned down a major permit that was required for them to proceed, and now he's dead."

"Dear Heaven! How can we help you?" Forrest responded.

"We believe Donald was sent out here in order to pressure him into reversing that decision. He insisted on having a meeting in our house here with a couple of tough guys who were pushing me around to the point that my husband and a sheriff's deputy had to remove them. And then he had the nerve to come back again, apparently planning to meet someone else here after we told him in no uncertain terms that he wasn't welcome. Anyway, our friend, the deputy, had us meet with their artist today to make drawings of Donald's couple of goons to show another possible witness. We wanted to ask if you or your husband could get one of Donald's campaign photos and send it to us here?"

"Of course we can. Give me your email address and we'll get it to you today. Oh, and Jennifer, send your artist's sketches here to us on the off chance that we may recognize them."

Alex added, "We can do that, but our friend the deputy also took photos of their driver's licenses. We'll send those as well. If they're known to you, we'll appreciate anything you can tell us about them."

"We'll do that, and don't hesitate to call on us if we can be of more assistance."

We ended the call with our promise to keep in touch about this situation, and to fill them in about the other case we were here for.

"What next?" I asked Alex.

"Tomorrow is still free if we want to take the pictures back out to Wanda."

"But there were already neighbors peeking through their curtains at the crowd of strangers on her front porch."

"Aye; maybe we should meet her somewhere else."

"I'll phone her at home after her quitting time."

By the time I called Wanda we had received an email from the Fulton County District Attorney's office with an attachment. "Alex, here's our picture of Donald." His campaign photo projected self-assurance and confidence.

"A far cry from the cowardly fellow we pitched out of our house."

I called Wanda's house early and left a message. She called back a little after two-thirty, "We finished cleaning early today and I've got to go to City Hall to drop off my utility bill, so do you want to meet me there?"

"Alex? Wanda wants to know if we want to meet her at City Hall this afternoon."

"Aye, that's a grand idea. And then ask her if there's someplace we can take her and treat her to someone else waiting on her."

Wanda said yes, there certainly was, she had a favorite bar where she sometimes liked to have a beer after work. "And how are you related to me again?"

"Gabe is the nephew of your sister-in-law; we're his aunt and uncle on the other side."

"Yeah, right. I'd better just stick that note you wrote in my purse. How long will it take you to get here?"

"An hour."

"I'll leave home in three-quarters of an hour."

We put Dragon in a run, left Monty in the house and took off in the motor home. The GPS took us right to the Benson City Hall and we spotted Wanda's little sedan. "You sure made good time; I just got here and dropped my bill in the box."

Alex grinned, "It always helps to have a badge tucked in next to your driver's license. You may not want to try that yourself."

"Oh, don't worry about it, for one thing, I'm too old to drive that fast. What did you want to see me about?"

"The driver's license photos of those two fellows were pretty awful, but we brought out the artist's sketches. Tell us where to meet you, and then we'll show you."

"It's only a couple of blocks. Follow me, if you can drive that slow."

It was only a couple of blocks; we parked and walked into a small restaurant and bar with dim lighting and country music playing. Wanda led us to a corner table away from the bar and under a fluorescent light fixture that appeared to be burned out.

"Hey, Wanda," the bartender yelled, "You're not sitting at the bar today? What, you're too good for us now?"

"Got some shirt-tail relatives in town I'm showing around. Three *cervesas* here, okay?"

The bartender brought three foaming mugs. "So where you folks from?"

"Canada," Alex answered.

"Well, this is a good time for you to be here. Been to the caves yet?"

"Last week." Alex told him. "We were totally impressed, it was awe-inspiring."

That apparently satisfied the bartender and he went back behind the bar. I had let Alex with his faint Scottish-Canadian accent do all the talking.

"Nosy SOB," Wanda observed. "So watcha got for me?"

I had brought along an oversized purse so I wouldn't have to fold the drawings. I pulled them out and slid them across the table.

"Oh, yeah, these are a lot better than those driver's licenses. Yeah, these are the two guys that came out with the cowboy from the developer."

"How about this one?" I pulled out the picture of Donald.

"Nah, I never saw that one. Just those other two."

"Wanda," I said, "those guys could be dangerous. We have good reason to believe the Webbs' deaths weren't accidental. If you should see them again, please be careful."

"Aye," Alex said, "call your nephew, Gabe, and if you don't get through to him, call my cell phone, or Jennifer's." He wrote all of our numbers on the cocktail napkin. "This is no joke, Wanda, those men *are* dangerous."

"No problem, I'm just a grumpy old waitress who should have retired years ago."

"Well, keep on your grumpy face, but call one of us. And this is our treat, so do you want another beer, and a police escort home?"

"Nah, one is my limit."

We all left the bar, Wanda waved at the bartender and said, "Seeya again next week," and Alex drove us back home.

"That was certainly informative," Alex said. "Now, we have: One, the comment you overheard; Two, the phone call of the congressman to Bryce Webb as repeated by his wife; and Three, an eyewitness who saw that pair of tough guys in the community where Mr. and Mrs. Webb died under suspicious circumstances. If we were back in San Diego I'd suggest cooking a meal for Madame District Attorney and Judge Davidson and ask if we had a possible criminal investigation."

"Lots of luck doing that here; the County Attorney's representative didn't recognize your name when I gave my deposition; she was skeptical when I told her no, you hadn't forced open that storage shed, the cop had, and when I mentioned your credentials she just shrugged it off. I think we have, as Madame District Attorney would put it, no standing at all."

"While we still have a pair of very suspicious deaths, and a good idea who is responsible."

"Maybe we can still do that dinner when we get back home, and ask our own very capable law enforcement team about the next step."

"I'm sure they'll be delighted at the prospect of another of your marvelous meals."

"We'll make it contingent on their showing us a path forward on this problem."

"Speaking of meals, what marvel do you have planned for us tonight?"

"I'll thaw some shrimp, there's another new recipe to try. And don't forget that we'll probably have to feed Robin over the weekend."

"He's always worth feeding; first for the information he's brought us in the past, and second, he may even come up with some useful ideas this time."

CHAPTER NINE
(*Friday, November 15 –Sunday, November 17*)

Our four days of dog shows this time were at the fairgrounds, the location I liked best of these November shows. The parking area was generous and we could usually count on at least half of the shows for our breed being indoors.

Monty needed one more leg for his Utility Dog title, and then he could relax at home while Dragon was our representative in the breed ring. One of the judges this weekend was a longtime friend and the club was offering special awards for any dogs finishing titles at that show. Linda was judging Utility on Saturday, the day that driving and parking were usually the most challenging. At least this year the bicycle race that was tied to the timing of the Thanksgiving weekend was a week later than our dog shows, and the construction project on our road down to the show site was finally finished.

Today Dragon was Best of Breed in the morning. With Group judging late in the afternoon we went back home for lunch after we found Robin and invited him for dinner. "Darling, I'm committed to the judge's dinner tonight, and I'm afraid I don't have any more gossip to trade you for a meal this time."

"Ah, but we do, Robin, and it's so good that after we tell you, we'll have to kill you."

"Ooh, I can hardly wait."

"I guess you'll have to wait until tomorrow."

With the turmoil caused by Donald and his goons, I hadn't really planned menus for our time here, so we stopped at the Safeway on the way home. The house was well stocked with staples, and this store always carried heirloom tomatoes so I picked out several of them and bought a pound of (previously frozen) shrimp for when Robin joined us for dinner.

I had called ahead to the pizza place around the corner from the Safeway and ordered a large one so I could have a slice for breakfast before Utility. We picked it up after we got our groceries, and sent Monty and Dragon out into the yard before they talked us out of my breakfast.

When we got back down to the fairgrounds for Group judging I looked over the other Herding Group representatives lined up at ringside and decided Dragon had an excellent chance at a placement today. He was still young and there were other dogs with more maturity, but I thought our chances were excellent. I hadn't shown to this judge before, but I'd seen his picture several times in our national magazine with dogs as well as bitches in winning photos, so I could be sure of at least an honest look.

I was so lightheaded when he handed me the Group First rosette that I worried about embarrassing myself by passing out in the ring. He noticed. "Take a deep breath, this is a magnificent dog. Don't embarrass me by passing out."

That made me laugh, and the lightheaded moment passed. Alex was waiting at the ring entrance and gave me a hug that almost took my breath away, and made me light-headed all over again. "Oh, wow! I just hoped for a placement."

We had to wait for the Toy Group to finish in the ring next to ours, and when a Chinese Crested went to the first place marker it was finally time for Best in Show.

"At least we don't have to wait while she grooms it," Alex joked as the little, hairless dog trotted over to our ring.

It would have been a fairy tale ending if Dragon had won Best in Show, but just a Group First was cause enough for celebration. We did get a really good look from the judge and I'd be sure to give him an entry if he judged our breed in the future.

"Shall we stop at the Safeway again for a bottle of champagne?" Alex asked.

"Two bottles, and save them for tomorrow so we can gloat to Robin."

Saturday morning I was back down there before eight in the morning so Monty could compete again in Utility with my friend as judge. I knew our friendship wouldn't give me a single point's advantage; she was dedicated to the sport of obedience and its integrity.

When we entered the ring she asked softly, "Jennifer, I was asked to take over an Open assignment as well as my own today because a judge died; had you heard anything about that last weekend?"

"Oh, did we ever! She and her husband may have been killed. When will you have a chance to talk?"

"Maybe a couple of minutes when you finish your exercise and we go over your score."

As we'd been talking Linda had been pointing to her judges' sheet with the list of exercises and the order in which they'd be performed. "Okay, are you ready?" She asked.

This time the smaller dogs went first and the stewards raised the jumps as the legs of our competitors grew longer. I was pleased with Monty's performance and as Linda went over the score sheet with me I filled her in on Janet Webb's untimely death.

"My husband was asked by the detective to visit the scene to see if anything might have been missed. Without taking the rest of your morning, it appears that her husband had pissed off some powerful people, and now they're both dead."

"How awful! Is anything being done?"

"Yes, and when we learn more we may be able to tell you more. It may have to be by email well after these shows are over."

"Thanks. I didn't know Jan well, but of course there's a small enough community of obedience judges that most of us have at least met a few times."

As I was leaving the ring the woman with the sable shepherd shoved past me at the ring entrance. "Do your bitching to the judge on your own time; don't hold the rest of us up."

Linda was close enough to have heard that and looked up. I smiled; books had been written about people's excuses for failing in the obedience ring: 'Someone called a dog with the same name in the next ring.' 'There must have been a bitch in heat.' 'The steward set the jump at the wrong height.' 'I'm sure the judge handled the scent article after I did.' 'There was too much noise while we were doing the Signal Exercise.'

I took a chair near the ring entrance to wait for our score. It would have been amusing if I hadn't felt sorry for the dog. Once again she failed scent discrimination; she acted as though she didn't know what was required, nosing around in the articles on the ground and then picking up one at random. The signal exercise was just sad. The poor dog went down on that signal, but then at the signal to sit, she took it for a recall command and trotted back across the ring to her owner, and got a firm "NO" for it. Linda shook her head and approached the woman to explain that they were non-qualified. I was seated close enough to the judge's table that I heard her say, "That woman in the ring before me interfered with us."

"How so?"

"You should have seen it for yourself; she blocked me from getting into the ring."

"You're supposed to wait until the steward calls your number. If you have a complaint you can file an objection." She smiled. "But don't forget that the steward and I will be called as witnesses."

The woman jerked the leash again as they left the ring, and when it was certain she had gone, Linda motioned to me. "What was that all about?"

"Last week she was drilling the dog in front of me at ringside and I spoke to her about it. This time she was pissed off that you and I were having a conversation. She seemed to think I was taking her time."

"Well, let's hope she doesn't decide that another judge needs to be eliminated."

I shook my head. "The poor, dead judge just happens to have had the bad luck to be married to someone that someone else wanted dead. You're probably safe."

Three more teams competed and then Linda called us back into the ring. We were rewarded when Linda read out the scores; a Border Collie outscored us but Monty was in second place. The woman with the shepherd was long gone, but the rest of us had all earned qualifying scores.

"Congratulations, all of you, and the club has a special award for anyone completing a title today. If you finished your title today, let me make a note on your score sheet and take it to the superintendent with my congratulations."

I grinned and handed back mine. "Monty finished; I wanted to give you an entry and say hello, and I hoped he'd get his last leg today."

She initialed our score card and returned it to me. "I've got to just keep going; they've really loaded me up today; I'm doing rally after Utility and that will take all my time until lunch."

As the rest of them left the ring Linda walked me out and asked,

"So what more can you tell me about Jan's death?"

"Have you heard anything about a ginormous development planned for a small town east of here?"

"I vaguely remember something on a national cable news show, but I probably wasn't paying attention."

"Well, a Fish and Wildlife official denied a key permit, there was apparently some pressure put on him by some higher-up officials, and then he and his wife died in a house fire. His wife was the obedience judge"

"How tragic. Could it have been just a coincidence? I sure hope so."

"I hope so too; I didn't know her, and we qualified under her replacement, but it was still sad."

Linda's schedule didn't allow for waiting for our photographer to come to the ring so I told her we'd get our photo later, hopefully with a breed photo as well.

I got back home to find that Alex had made another delicious second breakfast; a cornbread muffin mix with simple directions, but delicious. There weren't many crumbs left when we finished, but Monty, Dragon and Misty got to lick the plates.

Breed judging was midafternoon, leaving us enough time for a nice lunch and a drive back down to the fairgrounds. We left Monty in the little motor home for our photo later; if we hauled his crate to ringside while Dragon competed in the breed ring we could be sure he'd know he was being left out.

In the conformation ring we were once again competing against Verna Daly's male Special, and she didn't even bother to be polite. I remembered Robin's comment that she had stiffed him on a show photo.

We lined up for Best of Breed and Dragon was in front with the lower number.

"I see you finally got rid of your moth-eaten old dog."

"He was runner-up to High in Trial today to finish his Utility title. I didn't see any performance titles listed in the catalog for your dog."

"That's such a waste of time."

"Not really, but I guess it keeps you from having to get extra show photos that you won't pay for."

That touched a nerve, and as the judge motioned to us to circle the ring I didn't bother with the traditional, 'are you ready?' I started with Dragon and caught her off guard. She jerked her dog's lead as she followed us. Dragon was Best of Breed, and as I left the ring with Dragon's rosette she stepped right in front of me and said, "You sabotaged us on purpose."

"No, I just saved you the price of a picture."

"You repeat that libel and I'll sue you!"

I laughed. "Better get your terminology right first; it's not libel unless I put it in writing."

The show schedule stated that Group judging would begin at 2:15 in two large, adjoining rings to run two Groups at a time. "Let me find Robin and tell him we'll get our picture after Group. With luck we'll have more to brag about." We followed the public address calls of 'Photographer to Ring Eight' until we located him. "Robin, we'll head to your photo setup after Group for our photos. And then, come for dinner."

"You couldn't keep me away, darling."

All of the judges' assignments at these shows were different every day; in order to finish titles, dogs had to win championship points under at least three different judges. In obedience we had to earn qualifying scores under three different judges. The Group and Best in Show judges were also different faces every day; at those levels everyone wanted a piece of the action and if a judge was known to favor one breed or size, we all hoped for a better chance the next day.

This judge was someone I hadn't shown to before; his address in the premium list was in New England. A snowbird escaping winter, no doubt. But although we had different judges every day, most of them sat in the designated judges' section at the end of the day and saw what dogs their colleagues put up. Today had drawn the highest entries of the four-day weekend, there were nationally ranked dogs competing against us today and our chances were far slimmer. On the other hand, our judge had very likely seen Dragon win the Herding Group yesterday and wasn't likely to ignore him.

We made the first cut of six dogs which wasn't even worth bragging rights, but then we were in the final four, and finally third behind a German Shepherd grandson of the almost legendary Angel Eyes and a lovely Border Collie bitch.

These days I didn't always get a Best of Breed photo, but with Dragon's success over this two week circuit it would be a good idea to flatter all of our breed judges with photos. And Linda, of course, for

Monty's final leg of his UD. Since the club had stocked up on trophies for dogs finishing titles without regard to championships, obedience or other titles, our award was a generic bowl. A nice bowl; since Arizona was known for its copper mining history, we got a copper bowl large enough to hold a few avocados or tomatoes that needed ripening.

"I'll see you at your house as soon as I finish here, darling," Robin told us.

We ate at the lovely, custom dining set that had been made for Kent and me by a small Mexican furniture store. I made a simple, but elegant dinner. Shrimp Singapura: sautéed shrimp on creamy white rice in a sauce of butter, fresh mushrooms, shallots, heirloom tomatoes and whipping cream. It was a delicious and pretty recipe, and insanely easy to prepare.

"While you cook I'll do your photos. After dinner, we'll gossip."

The dogs had been fed and sent out after their dinner. I let them back in as we made ourselves comfortable after our own. The dogs knew Robin and had occasionally begged a treat from him. There were no treats tonight, but Robin was also good for ear scratches. When Misty waddled in Robin looked up and said, "Oh My God! Do I need to wash the dishes while you whelp the litter?"

"Hopefully not; we should have more than enough time to get her back home after the shows, but Alex built us a whelping box here last week."

Robin handed the photos off to us. "On the house, darling, in exchange for that splendid feast."

"Robin, those were frozen shrimp; maybe worth one photo, but not all three."

"I thought you were planning to feed me more than once."

"Well, of course."

"Then keep these. If you do get Best in Show, you can pay for that one."

We sat around in the living room part of the 'great room,' in front of the large fireplace. It was too warm for a fire yet, but it made an attractive focal point for the room. I told Robin about the time our national club president had stayed here for the Board meeting prior to our Tucson National Specialty. "She has a Southern accent you can cut with a spoon; she looked at our fireplace and asked, 'Is that a *walk-in farplace*?' and I didn't have a clue how to answer. Luckily, one of our other members was able to translate for me, and her question was simply, 'was that a *working fireplace?'* and I agreed that it was."

That got laughter from Robin. "I don't have any gossip to trade you for that marvelous meal; I'll have to see if I can dig up something to trade for tomorrow's dinner."

"Ah, but this time we have the inside story to offer you," Alex said. "Here's what we know so far." And we filled him in on what we had learned to date.

"No working smoke detectors in the house? They died of smoke inhalation? I change our batteries twice a year with the change to daylight savings time; what do you do here where you don't have DST?"

Alex answered, "We check each unit every time we come over, there's a wee bit of tape stuck to each one with the date of the battery, and I always replace the oldest one. I can at least reach them with the step-stool; Jennifer would have to carry in the ladder."

"Well, I'm relieved that two of my favorite people, and definitely my favorite chef, are taking their safety and security seriously."

"Of course, and plan on coming again tomorrow."

"Oh, darling, you couldn't keep me away. And now I should get back and work on the rest of these."

On Sunday Verna Daly herself was nowhere in evidence at ringside. There was a man in a suit and tie holding her Special. The judge had just handed out final placements in Shelties and as they filed out of the ring, the handler forged ahead and took a position far enough across the ring that there was no room in front of him for Dragon, with the lower armband number. I'd been showing for enough years that this chicanery was nothing new. I paused at the ring entrance and pointed out our number to the steward. She hadn't noticed, but looked at the handler and then motioned to the judge. The two of them conferred softly and then the steward walked across the ring and asked the handler to move back far enough that we could take our position at the front.

I wasn't surprised when the handler moved close enough behind us to be almost nudging Dragon from behind. As the judge walked to the head of the line, I turned to the handler and said, "Would you move back a couple of steps? You're crowding my dog."

The judge looked up at us. "Yes, please leave a little more space between you and the dog in front."

The handler gave me a dirty look, but the judge was in command of his ring and he had no choice. The judge spoke again. "Once around the ring, first dog on the table."

I turned back to the handler, and asked loudly enough for the judge to hear, "Are you ready?"

He muttered, "Just get going."

So much for courtesy; I started off briskly and left him behind by the time we had covered a quarter of the ring. "Breed," he pointed at me, "and Opposite," as he pointed to Winner's Bitch.

The handler left the ring; Verna materialized and took the leash from him as he took off, presumably for another ring commitment. I asked the steward, "Can you see if Robin is available for a photo now, or if we should meet him at his setup later?"

She paged, "Photographer to Ring Six." I heard the answer, "Anything for you, darling," and being Robin, I couldn't guess whether he was answering the steward, or knew that it was our ring. We were feeding him, after all.

We were only sixteen miles from the house, it looked like we had close to three hours before Group; ample time for a nice lunch and a last check of ingredients for tonight's dinner.

"What haven't I cooked for Robin?"

"After all these years? Probably nothing. I have an idea; have you done your Chicken Suppositoria? If nothing else, Robin will be in convulsions over the history of that dish."

I had shown to our Group judge years before, with Monty, and we had done well. Not that I expected him to even remember me, and Dragon was a different dog of a different color. We filed into the ring in order, with Dragon next to last in line. There was no drama, no dirty tricks were evident, just the tension of hoping your dog was the one to make it to the Best in Show level.

It wasn't us, but we did end up with a piece of the Group, if only a fourth place. We got our photo at Robin's stand while the other Groups were going on, and then I told Robin, "We'll head home now so we can create a feast for you."

"When I finish here I'll stop at your Safeway and bring the wine."

As I expected, Robin couldn't stop laughing over the account of

Chicken Suppositoria, the culinary disaster when I was still learning to cook and didn't know the difference between a clove of garlic and a bulb of garlic. I assured him that one mistake of that magnitude was enough for a lifetime.

While the chicken cooked I fed the dogs. Monty and Dragon scarfed theirs right down, but Misty was far enough along that she had to be hand fed with some coaxing. Robin said, "Jennifer, darling, let me do that while you pay attention to our meal. I'd hate for some slip-up that sent our supper into the dog bowls."

All of my dogs knew and liked Robin and had often cadged treats from him at my dinner table. "Deal, Robin." I handed him the small bowl of sautéed chicken livers; a fail-safe for getting food into a reluctant eater. Not that Misty was at all picky; she was just too stuffed to have much room for food. After Robin went into Misty's room I removed the chicken from the pan, added the vegetables and started a separate pot of water for the spaghetti.

By the time I had everything almost ready to serve Robin rejoined us. "Jennifer, I could only get a couple of bites down her, and then she retreated back into her nest and started scratching at her papers. When is she due?"

"Friday is what we've planned for, but you know as well as we that first litters are unpredictable."

"Well, I'd suggest getting her home as soon as possible unless you plan to raise the litter here. Would you like me to take her temperature? I promise to wash my hands before dinner."

"Yes, thanks, Robin. Her room is half of our guest suite with a Jack and Jill bathroom between the rooms. There are a couple of thermometers in the medicine cabinet; use the one with K9 in black ink on the case."

When he came back in five minutes he said, "I think you're safe for another day or so, it's just over one hundred, but there's no doubt she's going to have puppies."

Canine gestation was roughly nine weeks (63 days), but that was the average for the species, from Great Danes down to the toy breeds. In our breed it was usual for bitches to whelp a day or two earlier than that.

Robin praised the dinner and thanked us for not serving the original. Once again we sat around the living room area. Monty and Dragon had been sent out to the huge back yard; Misty would get her exercise in the tiny yard off the guest suite. We left the doors to her room open so we could hear any significant noises, but aside from that initial rustling of papers, she seemed to have settled into her nest.

"I know Alex was pleased with the vet here when he gave that class in Pinal County two years ago, but back home I have Sandra's home number in case of any emergency. After Poppy's disaster I'll feel far better with Sandra just a phone call away. Maybe we should skip tomorrow's show and just go home."

"Aye, there'll always be another dog show, but we have big plans for these puppies. Robin, we haven't spun you the tale of our summer vacation herding sheep."

Alex was a superb storyteller and by the time he finished Robin was laughing so hard he finally said, "Stop, or I won't be able to drive back down to the fairgrounds."

We had gone to the ranch of friends in Alberta to help them put on our national club's first herding trial. Alex and I were volunteer help as clerks for the judges and timers, and as the event went on we became aware that the official times were being manipulated in favor of the people who had trained at the ranch in Montana that was holding another event following ours, or owned dogs bred there. While we were in Montana we helped the ranch owner solve the murder of her father and brother and prevent the murder of her son. And me; our villain had decided that I was also a threat to his plans and planned to drive the boy and me over a cliff with a flock of panicked sheep.

"Sheep? I always thought of them as sweet, gentle creatures. You made them sound almost menacing."

"Robin, first of all, they're BIG. When they were crowded around me their backs were as high as my waist. And then the ranch manager sent his dog to drive them at us with a raging river at our backs. My almost Best in Show dog drove them away from us, with the help of a couple of Border Collies. When it was all over I had nightmares of them with fiery red eyes, breathing flames as they charged at us."

"I may eschew lamb chops for the foreseeable future. They may come seeking revenge."

"Our dogs were impressive enough that we have several reservations for puppies to working ranches."

After Robin left we checked Misty's temperature one more time, and then went to bed. It was still over one-hundred; still likely that we had a few days before we had to help deliver puppies, but with her behavior tonight, cutting it too close for comfort.

CHAPTER TEN
(*Monday, November 18 – Tuesday, November 19*)

I let Alex cook up his fluffy pancakes once again while I readied the little motor home for our trip back to San Diego. Perishable foods went into the motor home fridge or house freezer; our laundry went into a storage area, and after breakfast the dogs went into their travel crates and we headed for home.

We got there after a long day, in the dark for the last couple of hours. By the time we crested the Laguna Summit the sun was sinking in the west and shining right into my eyes. That was the point where Alex took over the drive; he was tall enough that the sun shade blocked the glare and he drove the rest of the way home.

I had called ahead to Sandra's clinic and told her receptionist, Darlene, that we were on our way home and expected to be having puppies within the next few days. I had also called Marcus and asked him to walk over to the house and turn on some lights. "And then join us for dinner, do we have a story for you!"

It would have to be a dinner I could make with the ingredients at home or what we were bringing back with us.

Ginger-Gouda Beef; it was quick and easy and I could do it in my sleep. Which wasn't far from the truth tonight.

We unloaded the dogs, I fed them and settled Misty in our preferred whelping box. She settled in with a sigh and actually ate most of her dinner.

"Alex, Misty may have just given us a false alarm in order to come home to her own bed."

"I can't say that I blame her, but I'm also more comfortable having her home with your excellent vet. If she's comfortable tonight then we can also enjoy our own bed."

As we sat around my dining room table we told Marcus about the mystery swirling around our Tucson home. "Unfortunately, my brother-in-law seems to be right in the middle of this and we're not sure whether he's an unwilling dupe or a participant."

Marcus, as a purely impartial observer, wasn't inclined to cut my brother-in-law any slack. "I don't know the man, but I get a very bad vibe from everything you've told me about him. Admittedly I've only heard the stories from your point of view, but I don't find anything your Donald might say or do as trustworthy. It sounds to me that anything he does is for his own benefit, and damn the consequences. I'm sorry to have to say that about a member of your family..."

"Don't be, Marcus, after our last experience with him I don't trust him to tell the truth about anything."

"What can you do about it?"

"I don't know that there's anything we can do. Jennifer and I gave our friend, the sheriff's detective, as much help as we could, and now we're back here with puppies due, and we can hope that young Gabriel will be able to put together a strong case for homicide. And then there's the problem of charging those people who are now out of state."

Marcus thought for a moment and then asked, "Jennifer, do you think this is something that would interest Judge Davidson?"

"Oh, I'm sure he'd love it, but I'm not sure what even he could do."

Alex, however, had a different take on it. "If Clarke Davidson and Damaris Colton take an interest, something might just happen. If Madame District Attorney thinks it's worth pursuing she might help set wheels in motion in Atlanta. Why don't we invite them to lunch? "

"It's a great idea, if nothing else we'll have good company and get some ideas."

"At best, they'll want to get involved and we may be able to do something about the problem. Thanks, Marcus, you earned your supper tonight."

"Then pour me a drop of your excellent Scotch, and then I'll totter on home. You two have had a long day."

Alex poured three tiny glasses – with an ice cube in mine. Marcus swirled the glass under his nose, inhaled the aroma, took a sip and declared that it was superb.

"Balvenie, fourteen years, old man, it had better be."

It was an excellent Scotch; I fell asleep almost when my head hit the pillow.

In the morning Alex's mustache tickled my neck. "If you had done that last night I think I'd have hit you with something."

"No fear, I'm afraid my superpowers were left behind in the Mountain Time zone. I'm not sure if they've caught up with me yet."

After breakfast I phoned Damaris. It was early enough that she shouldn't have yet gone to court. "Jennifer, good to hear from you. Please don't tell me you've been in the way of another herd of rabid sheep."

"No, but we have another mystery; it's out of your jurisdiction, but we hoped to invite you and Judge Davidson to lunch and pick your brains. It will be our treat."

"Tell me." So I did.

"Good God! I've seen a bit of that controversy on the news, but I admit I didn't pay a lot of attention. Are you saying the death of that supervisor may have been murder?"

"Our friend, the deputy, thought something wasn't quite right and asked Alex to visit the scene with him." I told her what Alex had deduced from the crime scene – yes, I was now calling it a crime scene – and that the evidence supported that opinion.

"I'll call Clarke right away. I'm not in court myself today; I planned to observe a fairly new prosecutor, but I'll be sure to get away for lunch. Clarke can make our reservations; how many will we be?"

"Both of us, and I'm sure Marcus will want to join us. We told him about it last night. He's become our unofficial court reporter."

"Excellent, the court reporters are some of the most valuable members of our teams. Does noon work for you?"

"Absolutely. We'll be there."

The elegant dining room within walking distance of the courthouse was one of our favorite haunts. Though most of our meetings there were to discuss some legal problem, the food was excellent and often challenged me to try to duplicate it at home. Robert, the *maître d'*, had a phenomenal memory for important guests and just as keen an instinct aimed at privacy and confidentiality. I remembered the time Damaris told me, "He was trained by the CIA, you know." And when I stared at her, dumbstruck, she laughed and said, "The Culinary Institute of America." But I was never really certain that she was joking.

Damaris and Judge Davidson were already seated at the table in the small, private dining room. The judge stood up to greet us. "Jennifer, Alexander, and my old bailiff, Marcus! It's good to see all of you again; I hope today is just an information-seeking get-together and you aren't actively involved in this apparent murder."

"We hope so too, Your Honor, Clarke," Alex said. "We'd like to be able to steer our young friend, the recently promoted detective, to whatever resources might help him wrap up his case. I was very impressed that he followed up his suspicions, even when the first investigators on the scene wrote it off as accidental."

"Damaris gave me the thumbnail account as Jennifer gave it to her; tell me the whole story now while we wait for our lunch."

Alex and I took turns filling him in: my brother-in-law's insistence that he had to make his supporters believe he was a property owner in Arizona; the important meeting he had to hold in our home; the secrecy when his goons wanted me out of the house even while one of them was making suggestive comments to me and about me.

"So when Jennifer told me that one of them had laid hands on her I thought that having our friend the detective meet us at the house was a good idea. With Gabriel there we were able to get photos of their drivers' licenses. Jennifer overheard a somewhat suspicious conversation as they were hustling her out of our house. When we went to Benson for the Cavern tour a waitress in a local café gave us an earful of overheard conversations. We met her privately for even more information. The wife of the victim was a volunteer at the Caverns State Park so Jennifer arranged a meeting with the ranger who had been our tour guide and learned more interesting background. But the compelling argument for an arson fire was that every smoke detector in the house had been disabled."

"Wouldn't one of the victims have noticed that?" Judge Davidson asked.

"It was skillfully done," Alex told him. "Every battery had apparently been removed and put in again backwards, or simply left out. Maybe a single error like that could be explained away, but the victim was a government scientist and it doesn't seem likely that he would have been so incredibly careless, or even incompetent."

"And don't forget the vinyl siding," I added.

"Oh, aye, there were also a couple of stacks of siding panels leaning against the wall on either side of the patio exit from the bedroom. The toxic fumes from those could have incapacitated the victims and prevented them from escaping."

"You said arson," Damaris asked, "was there an accelerant?"

"Not that had been identified, but there were a couple of

cardboard boxes full of hot coals and embers, supposedly to look like someone had cleaned out the hearth. There had been some pretty cold nights; it made sense that they would have used the fireplace."

"But I'm hearing a 'but' in what you haven't told us yet," Damaris said.

"Madame District Attorney, do you have a fireplace?"

"Here in San Diego? Well, no, it would have just wasted wall space."

"Clarke?"

"Yes, there's one in my living room. It was an option when we bought the house and my late wife wanted one. She was from Colorado where everyone had a fireplace, and used it. I doubt we used ours more than once a year."

"So neither of you would be familiar with fireplaces. Ours up in Alberta sees a great deal of use during the winter. The firebox – the hearth if you will – is insulated so the heat is totally contained and can't ignite wallboard behind or around it, and ample space in front and to the sides so stray embers can't shoot out and ignite something in the room. Which brings us back to the victims' house. It was a very hot fire. When Gabriel first examined the scene there were still pockets of heat inside, the boxes of ashes next to the back door still held residual heat. What is telling about all that is that the firebox itself was totally cold; there had been no new fire in it even while there were hot embers in boxes by the door."

"Let me see if I processed that correctly," Judge Davidson said. "The hot ashes that may have started the fire didn't come from their fireplace, right?"

Alex smiled. "You hit the nail on the head. We asked Gabriel to review the autopsy results to see if there was something else that kept them from jumping out of bed and escaping the fire, but the combination of fireplace residue and disabled smoke alarms made me agree with him that this was almost certainly no accident."

Damaris had been listening, but making notes on a small pad of paper. "Can you identify that stack of siding?"

"Eh?"

"The siding. Were there any barcodes on the panels that hadn't been burned or melted off?"

"I can ask Gabriel. What's your thought?"

"Maybe they didn't buy those panels. Find out where they were purchased, if they were paid for by credit card, and whose credit card."

"Madame District Attorney, I think you're brilliant."

She grinned. "That's how I got this job. But seriously, I've read reports about that material that scare me. Product liability isn't something our office gets involved in, but I like to keep current. I've read some real horror stories about combustibility and toxic fumes from vinyl siding. I wouldn't want it on our house."

"Gabriel did tell me that one of the fire captains said they might as well have poured kerosene on the house."

"That's my impression. Have you talked to Detective Barrick about this? I hope the arson investigators are capable over there in small town Arizona, but Dan might be able to find you an expert to go over your evidence."

"We'll do that next, thank you, we knew this would be a valuable meeting."

Robert poked his head into the room. "Shall we serve your meals now?"

"Yes, thanks, I think our business is finished."

Lunch was as fabulous as ever and we left satisfied and well fed.

"Well, love, shall we plan a Crimestoppers meal around your table?"

"It sounds like a good idea, and it won't hurt to have Bonnie on hand if we end up with a whelping during dinner."

CHAPTER ELEVEN
(*Wednesday, November 20*)

Misty picked at her breakfast while I cooked ours, but at least if she was eating we probably had another day or so before her puppies arrived. Alex called Dan while I phoned Bonnie. Dan was the key to this plan but there was little chance that Bonnie would have other plans for dinner.

I heard Alex say, "Detective Dan, we have a new mystery that calls for some of your expert advice. Aye, tonight if you can, any later and we may be delivering puppies."

I called out, "Or Bonnie and I might be delivering them while you two solve our mystery."

I set up the whelping room with a grooming table to hold my supplies: soft, old kitchen towels to rub the newborns dry, hemostat and scissors to clamp and cut umbilical cords, a small postal scale to weigh each baby, and a chart to record weight, sex and color of each one. After all that was done, there was a small box lined with a towel over a heating pad so we could set aside the puppies already delivered while Misty worked on producing the next one. We hadn't had time to take her to Sandra for an x-ray to count puppies, but those late-date x-rays weren't one-hundred-percent accurate; there was always the possibility of the crowd of spines and skulls masking a hidden puppy. And, after this many years as a breeder I was pretty good at estimating the size of a litter.

"What do we want for dinner that's simple?"

"Steaks. Dan and I can take care of those if you and Bonnie get busy with Misty. Steak and potatoes will do very well; they already know how well you can cook."

Our dinner was a success; Misty's wasn't. She nosed her dish of chicken livers around and I later pulled it out from under a pile of her newspapers. Bonnie took her temperature while I was busy in the kitchen. "It's ninety-nine," she called out.

That was lower than it had been this morning. "We may get action tonight," I told everyone, "let's solve this mystery while we still can."

Dan took notes as we told him the story. "I agree with everything you've done, and I like Damaris' suggestion to try to trace the purchase of the vinyl siding. I've investigated a couple of fires involving that stuff and once it's ignited, it can really be deadly. Do you have any pictures of the structure?"

Alex scrolled through the images on his phone and handed it to Dan.

"Hmm, don't tell me I spotted something the Great MacLeod missed?"

"And what would that be?"

"What's left of the walls of the house are stucco; who puts vinyl siding over stucco?"

"Do you think maybe he got them to put on the barn?" I asked.

"In that case, I'd have expected to find them stacked at the barn," Dan answered. "I have an idea. Bonnie, is there enough of your cheesecake for one more person?"

"If I slice it thinner; who?"

"One of our top arson guys lives just a few minutes from here in La Mesa, I'll call and see if he can come over and brainstorm with us." He punched a number into his phone. "Hey, Gil, did I catch you at dinner? You've eaten? How about dessert? We're just a few minutes away with cheesecake, good Scotch, and an arson mystery. No, you don't need to bring anything, the mystery is over in Arizona, but I'm having dinner with one of the investigators and we could use your expertise...wait, I'll ask." He covered the phone. "What's the Scotch, MacLeod?" He turned back to the phone, "Balvenie ...okay, we'll see you soon." He disconnected and turned back to us. "He says that's one he hasn't sampled yet."

About fifteen minutes later the doorbell rang. Monty and

Dragon ran to the door, barking. Misty gave a half-hearted 'woof' from her room, but didn't make an appearance. I looked at Bonnie. "I hope we get through the cheesecake and Scotch."

Dan introduced Rocco McGill. "Everyone calls me Gil, do I have to solve your case before the cheesecake and Scotch?"

"Nah, we'll trust you. Bonnie would you get the dessert? Gil, this is the world renowned Alex MacLeod who will pour the Scotch."

I saw Alex wince, and then McGill said, "I've read your books. A little light on fires, but maybe I can give you a few tips for your next one."

Alex laughed. "Finally someone I can ask for an autograph."

"If you mention me in the credits you'll want to know how I came by such an interesting name," he said. "My mother is Italian, my Dad Irish, and when they get into a fight even I don't want to get between them." He was a large man; not as tall as Alex but with more bulk, and looked as though he had relaxed his workout routine some time ago. He also struck me as extremely mellow compared to his apparently volatile parents.

"I'll be happy to hear anything you can offer to help us." Alex summarized the story again. "The young deputy had recently made detective, the fire that took two lives had initially been judged an accident, but Gabriel wasn't satisfied and asked me to visit the site with him."

"Do you have any photos of the scene?"

Alex brought them up on his phone and passed it over.

"Any idea what the place looked like before it happened?" Alex shook his head. "Would you have a pad of paper and a pencil?"

Marcus said, "That's usually my job, I'll get them."

Gil took them from Marcus and using the pictures from Alex's phone he sketched the rear of the house as it must have been before the fire: a double sliding door from the master bedroom leading out to a patio. "Was the patio covered?"

"Aye, there was a roof of metal panels; they'd been knocked down and shoved aside when the fire crew was trying to put it out. I didn't photograph them but as I recall, they were green."

Gil added a bit to the sketch and then asked where the vinyl siding had been stacked and where the cardboard boxes of embers were located. When he finished he turned his sketch around so we could see it. "Here's how I reconstruct the scene." He had drawn a pair of sliding doors opening to a covered patio; he had drawn a stack of three or four siding panels on either side of the door leaning up under the eaves, and the shadowy outline of a box behind each stack of siding. It was an extremely talented drawing that made the house seem real as it grew on the page. "The vinyl siding was stacked on end so it reached up to the eaves and so led the fire right into the attic, or at least into the crawl space under the roof."

"If I'd been unloading a stack of siding panels I'd have just dropped them horizontally," Alex told him. "Someone went to some extra work to stack them on end."

"And lead the fire right up to where it could take hold. There should have been an accelerant to make sure of it; was there anything else found with those boxes of embers?"

"Gabriel said there was apparently a bag of kitchen trash also set out on that deck."

"Why put the kitchen trash out on the master bedroom deck?" Gil asked.

"More than that," I added, "In Arizona we don't set trash out to take it to the dumpster in the morning. There are coyotes and javalinas..."

"What are those?"

"Peccaries. Have you been to the San Diego Zoo?"

"Oh, yeah, those little piggy characters. The tour guide on the bus told us to look to our left to see Gregory Peccary."

"They're actually quite nasty and destructive. They can knock over large trash cans; they've been known to attack people. Plus, in that county it's illegal to feed the wildlife including being careless with pet food and trash that they can get into. It doesn't seem possible that a government wildlife supervisor and long-time resident wouldn't know that."

"Did their investigators list what was in that kitchen trash?"

"I doubt it," Alex answered, "they wrote it off as an accident from the start."

"You might try to find out; I still want to find an accelerant. It's just too chancy to hope a box of hot ashes will burn the house down."

"Do you think it's possible that they just wanted to intimidate him?" I asked. "They may have still needed him to sign off on that permit."

"I don't know anything about what's going on out there and I can't get inside anyone's head, all I can do is tell you how fires behave."

"You've given us something more to investigate and we thank you," Alex told him, "and I'll definitely ask for your help with my next book."

"I'll look forward to it, and here's my phone number. Call me if you think of anything else to ask, and definitely call me if you're able to locate an accelerant. If you find it, I can probably tell you more. Thanks for the dessert, and you've excellent taste in Scotch." He left; Bonnie and Dan went to load the dishwasher.

Bonnie went into my office and took Misty's temperature again. "Jen, it's dropped another degree; do you want me to stay in case you need help with the whelping?"

"Thanks, but if we can't handle it, it will probably be time to call Sandra."

They went home; Alex went into the office/puppy room and opened up the sofa bed. "Should these sheets be changed?"

"Oh, yes; I can't remember the last time this bed's been used." I put Monty and Dragon to bed in their crates, not without a dirty look from Monty. "Sorry, big guy, you're not needed here tonight, and they're not even yours." Luckily, dogs didn't understand most of our language.

When I got back to the puppy room Alex had brought both pillows from our bedroom. "You're joining me?"

"Of course. We may not be able to get frisky tonight, but at least we won't be lying awake, alone, in lonely beds. If this is a false alarm, we can at least curl up together and stay warm."

"Oh, we'll need a blanket or two as well." We both went to bed wearing warm pajamas, and while Misty gave us some background noise rustling and scratching papers it wasn't long until we fell asleep.

We woke to the familiar sound of a squealing newborn pup. By the time we got our wits about us, untangled the bedding and turned on the lights, Misty had cleaned that one and was working on a second.

Once she started she continued in a business-like way that made Alex and me almost redundant. We clamped and cut cords so she didn't cause an umbilical hernia in any of the puppies, rubbed them dry, weighed each one and wrote a description on my puppy log, and then tucked them aside in the warm box while Misty continued with her delivery. By the time the sky outside was getting light she had six plump puppies, five females and one male. A dream ratio considering the number of females we had requests for. She managed the whole process in a little less than three hours so we'd actually had more sleep than usual in these circumstances. We even had an attractive variety of colors; brindle Dragon and tri-color Misty had produced all possible colors except merle, and we knew very well that they couldn't produce merle.

I put a leash on Misty and took her out to the front yard while Alex removed and bagged the soiled newspapers. And then we tucked the puppies into the whelping box, now lined with fresh papers and topped with a square of indoor-outdoor carpet on top of a heating pad, covered the box with a blanket, and left her in peace with her new brood.

CHAPTER TWELVE
(*Thursday, November 21*)

We showered and I made a simple breakfast. In spite of not being up all night as so often happened, we were still tired and intended to have a slow and lazy day, with the possibility of a nap later on.

I called my vet, Sandra Spaulding, and reported in. "A lovely litter, she didn't need any help, what we were doing was mostly busy work. When do you want to do dew claws?" Those vestigial extra toes, usually only on the front feet, that were customarily removed in our breed.

"How are their weights?"

"All between ten and twelve ounces."

"Nice and sturdy; we may as well do them late tomorrow. Bring them in after closing."

There wasn't anything else we really had to do today so we loafed, and we napped, and we checked on the puppies every couple of hours. I stripped the bedding from the sofa bed and closed it up again. Alex said he was going to call Deputy Gabriel and ask him again about the accelerant Gil wanted us to find. I heard him ask, "You said there was a bag of household trash found next to the box of ashes; can you find out what was in the trash? Thanks, man, we had an arson expert for dessert last night and he had some questions." I heard him laugh. "You're right; he'd have taken a lot of tenderizing. Thanks, we'll be home pretty much all day today and tomorrow until we have an appointment with the veterinarian after five o'clock."

When it came time to feed the dogs Alex took Misty out to the yard again while I weighed each puppy. We expected newborn puppies to gain an ounce or more every day and to double their birth weights at the end of the first week. I was happy with their weights and when Alex brought Misty back in I made her a dinner of chicken livers that she gobbled down this time.

After Monty and Dragon had been fed I started the meal I had planned for the night over in Tucson when I couldn't find one of the key ingredients; Orange Marmalade Chicken. I sautéed the chicken breasts in butter, then asked Alex for the Grand Marnier. I grasped a wooden match with the kitchen tongs and poured in a generous splash of the liqueur. At that point Alex was supposed to ignite my match from the butane match we used to start the barbeque and I would then drop in the flaming match. But the pan was so hot it didn't wait for Alex's help; it went up in flames with a Whoosh that almost reached to the range vent. I jumped back and so did Alex. He grabbed the fire extinguisher from the wall next to the fridge, but by then the flames had died down to just a slow burn in the pan.

"Are we still looking for an accelerant?" I joked.

"That would certainly do the job," he answered.

Orange Marmalade Chicken

4 chicken breasts
½ stick butter
One 11-oz. can mandarin oranges
One cup chicken bouillon
One Tbsp. orange marmalade

Zest of one orange
¼ cup Grand Marnier
1 Tbsp. flour
1 Tbsp. lemon juice

Sauté chicken in butter until nearly cooked through, remove to baking dish, drain excess dripping from skillet. Add Grand Marnier to skillet and ignite. Allow flames to die down, add chicken bouillon, stirring to deglaze pan. Drain mandarin oranges reserving oranges and 3 Tbsp. juice. Combine flour with reserved orange juice, lemon juice and marmalade in small bowl and mix well. Add to skillet with orange zest. Cook until thickened, stirring constantly. Spoon sauce over chicken, add mandarin oranges, bake @ 350 for 20 minutes.

Serves four

From *Wild Thyme and Other Temptations*, compiled by the Junior League of Tucson.

CHAPTER THIRTEEN
(*Friday, November 22*)

It was halfway through the morning when the phone rang. Alex was closest and answered it. "Ah, Gabriel, do you have any news for us? Wait a minute; let me put it on speaker so Jennifer can listen."

Gabriel told us, "I went back to the scene and went dumpster diving."

"I hope you were wearing old clothes," Alex told him.

"Oh, yes, that's one of those mistakes you only make once. I put on a haz-mat suit. Even so, if it had been summer I would have smelled so bad my wife wouldn't have let me in the house. So here's what I found that I believe was in that bag of trash: the singed remains of a couple of paper plates and paper napkins, a greasy pizza box from a local restaurant, some waxed butcher paper and an empty liquor bottle."

Alex was nodding his head as Gabriel listed the items. Remembering last night's near-disaster I asked, "What was the liquor?"

"Something that looked fancy and expensive, but there wasn't anything left in the bottle to test for any kind of drug. It was a Grand Marinara or Marney-air..."

"Oh, my God!"

Alex knew exactly what I meant, Gabe asked, "What?"

"Gabe, I almost burned down our kitchen last night with a splash of that same liqueur – it's pronounced Gran Marn-yay – it's French, it's eighty proof, and it ignited in my skillet in a ball of flame before we could even drop in a match."

"Holy cow! So if there was anything left in that bottle it might have helped start the fire."

"It's worse than that, I was going to make that dinner when we were over there. I thought I had a full bottle, but it was missing."

"Gabe, lad, can you get fingerprints from that bottle?"

"I can try; I wore gloves for my diving expedition for obvious reasons. The bottle had broken; I had to fit the pieces together to read the label."

"Gabe, I took fingerprints from the glasses used by those unwelcome visitors to our house If you can get useable prints from that bottle and they match, we may have enough evidence for you to follow their trail back east."

"Superintendent MacLeod, is there any possibility you could come back here and compare the fingerprints yourself? I'm just not sure enough of my own skill."

Alex looked at me and ra sed an eyebrow; how could he do that so eloquently when if I tried it I just looked like I had a nervous tic? I nodded, and he turned back to the phone. "I can probably get a flight today. We just had puppies Wednesday night so we can't both be away. I'll call you with my flight information. You will? Well thanks, that should save some time." He put the phone back and turned to me. "I hate to do this, lass, but if what we're starting to suspect is true, you may have had a pair of killers in your house."

"Of course, there's nothing here I can't handle."

"What about your appointment with the vet?"

"I managed for years on my own, but Marcus is always willing to help out."

There was a flight he could catch before noon which would give me more than enough time to drop him off at the airport and get back in time to take the puppies to Sandra.

While we were on our way to the airport he phoned Rocco McGill and reported on the possible accelerant. I heard the voice through the phone, "Oh, man, I wish I could go there with you."

"Why don't you? The flight wasn't full when I called and your badge should get you through security without an hour or more wait."

I dropped Alex off at the airport and drove back home again. This trip was certain to be at least an overnight and normally I would have gone with him, but not with newborn puppies. Sandra's office manager, Darlene, called me a few minutes before five o'clock and told me the last appointment was just finishing up. I called Marcus, and then weighed each puppy as I tucked it into the soft airline carrier. Since Sandra would weigh them herself this would show me how close my little postal scale was to her more accurate one. I put Misty in a crate in the back of the van, Marcus climbed into the passenger seat and we drove the short mile to the clinic. Marcus' assignment was to walk Misty around in the small yard behind the clinic and distract her from the fact that we were tormenting her puppies inside.

Sandra examined each puppy, checked my chart with sex, markings and weight and weighed each one herself. "When did you weigh them last?"

"As I was loading them."

"Good, your scale is accurate." She proceeded to remove the extra toes with a little, glowing wire loop that not only removed the vestigial toes, it cauterized the tiny wound. She finished the process with a drop of vet glue and then we checked each pup once again. There were no rear dew claws so each pup sported a tiny drop of blue glue on the front feet where the toes had been. "All done," she said, and we took Misty and babies back home. Once they were all back in the box she rolled and scrubbed them to remove every trace of hospital stink.

"I didn't have time to ask you," Marcus told me, "where's Alex?"

"Back in Tucson. We had a revelation last night when we almost burned down our kitchen. Do you want to stay for dinner so I can tell you about it?"

"Of course, but should I go home and bring over my fire extinguisher?"

"No, I won't flambé anything tonight. How about a simple meatloaf? I'll even send the leftovers home with you."

"Of course."

I fed the dogs while the meatloaf baked. Misty had a normal meal of kibble and canned dog food with a scoop of meatloaf gravy. I no longer had to tempt her appetite; now I just had to keep her filled as she ate for seven.

I filled Marcus in on what we had learned since our Wednesday evening dinner. "It was a bottle of Grand Marnier, eighty-proof, that almost set the kitchen on fire, and I had planned that same recipe for us over there, except that I thought I had a full bottle, and it was missing."

Alex phoned late, after Marcus had gone home. "We had a very productive day, Gil is staying at the house here, and we're going to do more detecting tomorrow."

CHAPTER FOURTEEN
(*Saturday, November 23*)

Alex gave me a full report, almost word for word, so I can narrate his trip over there almost as well as if I had been there. He described the near-disaster in our kitchen on the flight over. Gabriel met them at the airport and drove straight out to the crime scene near Benson. The evidence had been secured; Alex supervised while Gabe lifted the fingerprints from the Grand Marnier bottle and then guided him through the comparison with the prints from the glass in our house. "Of course I could lift the prints myself, but this is your case, and if you finally take it to court you don't want an outsider with no jurisdiction to be involved with any of the evidence."

Gil went over the site from every angle. He first took video, then measurements and examined the evidence: the mostly-melted panels, the remains of the cardboard boxes, the bag of household trash. When he said he was satisfied, Gabe drove them back to our house. Nearly there they passed our local Rural-Metro fire station – the place where I had dropped off the small rattlesnake years ago.

"Hold it!" Gil said, "Pull in there for a minute." As they all got out one of the fire fighters called out, "Can we help you?"

"I need to burn down a house," Gil hollered in reply. "Have you got someplace I can practice?"

"You want we should arrest you now, or later?"

"You might want to wait until we've proved our theory. We could have someone else to arrest."

They held a brief conference and Gil explained how he wanted to duplicate the circumstances of a probable arson fire. It was a slow day at the fire station and the guys joined in enthusiastically. Yes, there was a practice site, a boxy, cinder block structure where they could try to duplicate the elements of the fire. "Wonderful," Gil said, "we have to buy some of the suspicious components, and we need some hot fireplace embers."

"You can use our barbeque," one of the fellows said, "as long as you give it back by dinner time."

"If we take too long we'll order pizza," Alex told them.

They went shopping. "Gil was having a wonderful time with our credit card," Alex told me. "Lowe's for the vinyl siding, but also two-by-sixes for eaves and roof supports and drywall over those. Next to Safeway for paper plates and napkins, in paper bags, naturally, and the star of the show, the Grand Marnier. When Gil saw that it was twenty-five dollars a bottle he asked if we should pass it around among us first." They bought pizzas for the crew at the station and after they polished off the first sausage, pepperoni and mushroom they kept the greasy box for the fire.

In the morning they built a roof over the practice structure with the wood supports and nailed up drywall inside to make a ceiling. "We need an air space above the ceiling for the fire to spread," Gil said. "I don't suppose you want to buy a set of roof trusses, do you?" he asked Alex.

"My wife will certainly question the credit card bill if we do," he answered.

"Well, I guess we can nail another layer of drywall on top; we just need to create an air space for the fire to spread." With Alex and Gabe's help he stacked the siding panels vertically on either side of the opening that served as a door. Part of the fire crew had joined us there to watch the exercise – and put out the fire if it got out of control. They brought the station's portable grill, and when the briquettes were glowing the fellows scooped them into cardboard boxes, tucked one under the panels on each side, put the paper trash bag full of paper trash next to a box of embers, and finally uncorked the bottle of Grand Marnier.

Alex called me when they broke for lunch with the rest of the pizzas, also on our credit card. "It went up with as satisfying a whoosh as what happened in our kitchen. It traveled up the siding panels to the eaves and spread through the airspace in only a couple of minutes. We didn't try to breathe the air inside; we took the word of the experts that the fumes were toxic. All in all, it was an impressive reconstruction of that fatal fire and Gil took video of the whole process. After we finish the pizza Gabe is going to check into the origin of the siding panels. We know which home improvement store they came from, he got a warrant for the sales receipt information, he'll pick that up sometime later today or tomorrow. We've got a flight home that gets in about five this afternoon. Do you want to meet me, or should I take the shuttle...oh, wait, Gil says he has his car at the airport, he'll drop me off."

"Shall we feed him?" I heard a muffled exchange and then Alex said, "He accepts, but we'll send him home early."

"What about Dan and Bonnie?"

"If they're free; it could be an interesting evening. But we'll still send everyone home early."

I called Dan and when he heard about Alex's trip to Arizona he said they were definitely free. I quickly paged through my cookbook of favorite recipes for something easy that would stretch for a crowd. Hunter's Stew fit the occasion; a simple, one-pot meal that basically cooked itself, and I had all the ingredients on hand. Well, almost all. I called Alex's cell phone; it went to voice mail so I just left a message. "Before you leave, cut a generous sprig from the bay tree and bring it back." We had a lovely bay tree outside the Tucson house that I had planted from a five-gallon pot when my late husband bought the house; it was now a substantial shrub. I hated to use herbs from a grocery store bottle when we grew most of our own.

Dan and Bonnie were already here when Gil and Alex pulled up to the house a little after six. Bonnie and I had fed the dogs and weighed and admired the puppies. Our dinner had been gently simmering for most of an hour and as soon as Alex brought me the small branch he had pruned from the bay tree I dropped in a couple of leaves. "With what you brought back I could almost plant another tree."

"Now that sounds like an excellent idea. Can you make this one take root?"

I had done that with a cutting from a rosemary bush at the Tucson, but rosemary plants grew like weeds all around Tucson. I didn't think I could be that lucky with an actual small tree. "I doubt it, but we can go to the nursery and get one to plant."

"Be sure no one mixes up your bay leaves with oleander leaves," Dan said. That was in reference to a situation several months ago when friends had asked me to do a welfare check on an elderly, retired AKC judge. We ended up unmasking a serial killer who had been preying on elderly people as a home health aide for at least a decade. She had disguised all those deaths as mishaps by confused old people accidentally including poisonous substances in their cooking. One of those mishaps had been the replacement of the bay leaves in a commercial bottle with oleander leaves. Since Dan had been the arresting officer in that case, he made it a point to inspect the bay cutting before I tossed the leaves into our stew.

Marcus walked over when he saw Gil's truck pull in. "Am I your court reporter again tonight?"

"Absolutely, old man, we couldn't get along without you."

Gil had used the hour-long flight back here to refine his sketch.

"That's really good," I told him. "It almost makes the house come to life."

"I was an art major in college. Then I joined the service and learned all about fires and things that go bang. One of the things that helped make me an expert was being able to reconstruct the scene on paper so I could give jurors or investigators a real picture of the scene. Anyway, after I had a look at the actual scene we went back to your fire station and recreated it. If you have a laptop you can set up here we'll have dinner and a movie."

It was an impressive movie and the bottle of Grand Marnier performed even better than it had in our kitchen.

Gil turned to me. "Alex described your flambé, and I agree; Grand Marnier makes an impressive accelerant. I may have to test a few more liqueurs."

"Count me in," Dan said with a grin. "And what about fingerprints? Wasn't that why you went over in the first place?"

"Aye, and I'm glad Gabe asked me. It was a difficult job; the bottle had broken, possibly from the heat, and all the apparent combustible material had been pitched away from the bedroom doors. He was able to get a couple of partial prints and they matched prints on the cocktail glass we believe was handled by the subordinate goon."

I wasn't even really surprised, but it gave me a chill nonetheless. "So Donald's important people are no better than murderers."

"True, and we don't want Donald or any of his minions in our home or anywhere near it again."

"More important, now we need to find and charge them," Dan said.

"It may be time to call on our friendship with the Atlanta District Attorney," Alex answered.

"And it can't hurt to ask for advice from our own DA," Dan said.

"I can call her Monday," I said. "But it sounds like an uphill battle to charge those guys with anything when they're back on the east coast now."

"Forrest Willoughby will certainly be able to help us with the Atlanta connection; we'll call both of them on Monday."

Our guests all left and we went to bed. Alex wrapped his arm firmly around me. "I feel the hair on the back of my neck standing up just thinking of those murdering sods in the house with you. If Donald or anyone associated with him comes anywhere near anyplace you are, call 911 immediately."

"I don't even intend to take his phone calls from now on."

CHAPTER FIFTEEN
(*Sunday, November 24*)

The phone rang when we were still asleep. At least it was Alex's cell phone, on the nightstand within reach, not the house phone down the hall.

"What the hell...?" I mumbled.

"MacLeod....WHAT? Gabe, repeat that, we weren't awake yet. That's right; we're an hour earlier here. Oh, shit! That puts a whole new face on it. Yes, I agree you need to proceed. Let me wake up and call you back when I can think clearly."

"What?" I asked.

"Gabe got the sales receipt for the purchase of the siding panels. They were paid for with Donald Roth's credit card."

"Dear God! I hoped my sister's husband was simply stupid enough to have been taken in by those goons. He may have been an active participant in murder."

"Aye, it begins to look that way. I think we'll give Forrest Willoughby a call today."

"And Damaris tomorrow; it looks like we're going to need all the legal guidance we can get."

We showered and I started breakfast while Alex called Gabe back. I listened to his side of the conversation as he confirmed that my brother-in-law had paid for the vinyl siding panels that had fueled the fire that killed the Fish and Wildlife supervisor – and our obedience judge.

Next, Alex called the Fulton County District Attorney. "Good morning, Muriel, this is Alex MacLeod. Is your husband available?"

He had turned on the speaker phone and I heard her response. "Alex MacLeod! Have you called with news about your investigation?"

"Aye, and this time it's looking more grim."

"Well then, you do need Forrest, and he's pruning the roses with Sal. Or watching while Sal prunes the roses. I'll call him."

I listened to both sides of the conversation as Alex and Forrest discussed the procedure for filing criminal charges against someone in Georgia for a crime that took place in another state.

"The young detective who removed Jennifer's brother-in-law asked for my help investigating a fatal home fire that was designed to look like homeowner carelessness but that he suspected was arson. It turned out that it was arson and we're following the trail of crumbs back to your fine city. The problem is, there's enough evidence to at least question our suspect, but not enough for an arrest warrant yet."

"How did you follow the trail back here?"

"I'm sorry to say Jennifer's brother-in-law seems to be up to his neck in it. We don't have enough evidence yet to file charges but we'd certainly have enough to bring h m in for questioning, except that he's now back in your jurisdiction, not ours. Oh? Well that would be marvelous. I'll talk to our Arizona detective, but I'm sure he'll agree; we'll send you all the information we have so far." He was smiling when he hung up the phone. "Forrest suggested that the county might just want to send the detective back there to do the questioning, and his office will supply all necessary assistance. In other words, he's not exactly a fan of Donald's."

CHAPTER SIXTEEN
(*Monday, November 25*)

When I got to the office I called our District Attorney. "Damaris, we have an interesting situation involving a homicide; it happened in Arizona and the suspects are now back on the east coast. It's worth buying lunch for you, and Amber if she'd like to join us, while Alex is still here to fill you in on the details."

"Girlfriend, there's nothing like a good homicide to give me an appetite, especially if I don't have to prosecute it. If your gorgeous husband is buying, I'll bring my appetite. The court calendar is pretty clear this week; I'm free whenever Amber is."

My boss's wife was also free this short, pre-holiday week. "And I'll even take care of our reservations," she told me.

The lunch special was Beef Wellington with new potatoes, and raspberry cheesecake for dessert. "I go back on my diet the second week in January," Damaris said. She was what was gently called a 'plus size,' but carried her weight well. I knew that at most of our lunches she just looked longingly at the exquisite desserts, but this time of year was basically an eating season and we'd probably all do penance later.

Between Alex's storytelling and the video on the laptop we brought along, it was a successful lunch. Over the cheesecake Damaris volunteered that Forrest Willoughby was right; a jurisdiction as large as Pima County could afford to send a representative to question the possible suspect, and if it were her call she'd send the young detective who figured it out in the first place.

Before we called for the check Damaris asked Robert, the *maître d'*, to join us in the small, private dining room. "Robert, do you ever flambé in the kitchen here?"

"Occasionally, and of course I do in my own kitchen."

"There was a fatal fire in Arizona, apparently with Grand Marnier as an arson accelerant. Watch this short video and give us your opinion."

Even so, he was too much of a professional to sit at the table with us, but tipped the laptop screen so he could watch while standing.

"In your experience, does that look like an accurate example of the flammability of the liqueur?"

"Absolutely, Ms. Colton. We had a range hood scorched in this kitchen when a new sous chef ignited a volatile liqueur. When it blew up just like that, the idiot turned on the fan. We were closed for several days for the only time in our history."

"I hope he learned his lesson."

"If so it would have been in someone else's kitchen; his resume was apparently a bit inflated."

I was certain the unfortunate sous chef had been sacked on the spot without a reference. I might be forgiven for almost burning down our kitchen; a trained chef wouldn't be.

CHAPTER SEVENTEEN
(*Thanksgiving*)

After our feast I had to see Alex off back home with Belladonna's puppies due early next week. The saddest thing about sending him home – aside from not having his head on the next pillow – was not having anyone to share the turkey leftovers. The leftover recipes were the best part of the turkey as far as I was concerned.

"We'll figure it out, lass. If you can't get Mandy to puppy-sit I'll get a vet or aggie student to stay with Belladonna's litter."

"The turkey leftovers will be here, don't forget."

"I'm not likely to forget where the turkey is, but you might try to arrange a trip up north to take a look at our second litter. Didn't we say we wanted to do a round-robin with all the puppies we have coming?"

True; we had not only our two litters, but puppies owed to us from Mandy's Monty daughter, Champion Bonita, and Melanie Volmer's Champion Ruthie. And, not to be forgotten, Myrna Watson's lovely blue merle champion Haida in whelp to Alex's nephews' stunning tri-color, Champion Frodo, and due in about two weeks. While we had no claim to Mrs. Watson's puppies, we were sure each of us would want a new youngster that wasn't the offspring of one of our own dogs. All of these litters were related, but by trading some of the puppies around we could avoid keeping puppies too closely related to the ones that lived with us.

The usual suspects joined us for Thanksgiving dinner: Dan and Bonnie, and Marcus, for turkey, stuffing, cranberry jelly and candied yams. Bonnie brought the dessert and made the salad, and while everything was still cooking she and I fed the dogs, snuggled and weighed the puppies. I printed the pedigrees of the five litters we were considering and she studied them while the fellows discussed murders and arson. Dinner was a success. During our previous dinners we had just about talked the Arizona arson to death, this time we just relaxed and enjoyed each other's' company. The puppies in my home office and due around both of our countries occupied most of our conversation.

Dan and Bonnie cleaned up while Alex and I put away the leftovers, and we finally sent everyone home, checked on the puppies one more time, and crawled into our king-sized bed.

Taking Alex to the airport was never something that brightened my day but it was a hazard of our long distance, international marriage. Belladonna's litter was due any time in the coming week and while the veterinary student staying at the house might be as capable as either of us, there was no substitute for the breeder being part of the delivery of a new litter.

CHAPTER EIGHTEEN
(*Wednesday, December 4*)

There were two messages blinking on the answering machine when I got home. The first was an unfamiliar number with an Arizona area code, the second was Alex's and I was sure his news would be puppies.

When I played them back the first one was from Gabriel. "Mrs. MacLeod, is Superintendent MacLeod still with you over there? I have news from my trip back to Atlanta."

Alex's message said, "We have a gorgeous litter, call me as soon as you're comfortable."

I was pretty sure Alex would want Gabriel's news when I called him so I called Gabe's number first. "Mrs. Macleod, I need to talk to your husband, but this is something you need to know too. Your friend in Atlanta was wonderful; I see what they mean by Southern hospitality. He had arranged my hotel, had someone meet me at the airport, and after I interviewed your brother-in-law they had me out to their house for a wonderful meal."

"I'll bet Hallie didn't share the recipe."

"No, and I would have loved to ask my wife to try to cook it. But aside from those great parts of that trip, my interview with your brother-in-law was troubling. Of course he denied all knowledge of the fire and the death of Mr. and Mrs. Webb, but when I pointed out that his credit card paid for the siding panels that were one of the primary fuels of the fire, he claimed that you had asked him to buy those for you."

"He WHAT?"

"That's right; he said you asked him to buy them for you."

"That son of a bitch! Sorry, Gabriel."

"Don't be sorry, that was my reaction too."

"I'm supposed to call Alex – he's back in Alberta this week – but why don't you call him first and tell him that awful news. Then we can figure out what to do about it." I gave him both Alex's home and cell numbers.

I was sure Alex would call me as soon as he got off the phone with Gabriel, but I was furious at my duplicitous brother-in-law. It wasn't enough that he was somehow involved in a plot to pressure an official into issuing the permit for a major development planned by one of his congressional backers, when that plot turned to murder, he was willing to try to shift the blame to me.

When Alex called I was still fuming. "Damn Donald! If there's one thing we can count on it's that he'll always deny responsibility for anything that could reflect badly on him."

"Aye, that certainly makes my news take a back seat."

"Well, no. Tell me about the puppies and then we can take turns cursing Donald."

"We have six; four females, two males, with a nice mix of colors. She delivered them all last night and finished in time for me to have a good night's sleep. Can you get Mandy to stay with your litter and come up this weekend? Then we can plot what to do about your brother-in-law."

"I'll check with her. If she can't, they're doing well enough that they could go to Bonnie for the weekend."

I called Mandy, and yes, she was free. "Bon-Bon isn't due for three more weeks. We could have Christmas puppies."

"Do you have any idea how many yet?"

"She's not very big, maybe four."

Our arrangement had been that we would co-own the Monty daughter, Ch. Brookside Bonita, Mandy would train and show her, and I would get a puppy back when she was bred. The sire of the litter, Mandy's own home-bred champion, was totally unrelated to the rest of our line, and would give us a good outcrossed puppy to trade as we figured out which puppies would work best for which breeders.

In the morning I made flight arrangements for Friday morning. Marcus would drive me to the airport and then watch for Mandy to show up after school. With that done I called our District Attorney. "Damaris, you won't believe the turn our Arizona homicide has taken! Our friend, the deputy, questioned my wretched brother-in-law who claimed I had asked him to buy the siding panels that helped fuel the arson fire."

"Why, that son of a bitch!"

"My reaction exactly."

"Were you even in Arizona at the time of the fire?"

"Yes, I drove over that Monday; Alex flew in the next morning at the time Donald's 'important backers' were in our house and I overheard one of them tell Donald to get that Fish and Wildlife guy to change his decision and get their permit issued. So the fire hadn't happened yet on Tuesday, and on Friday I had a replacement judge at the dog show because our judge had died."

"Next question; when, exactly, was the receipt for that stuff dated? I mean date, and time of sale."

"I don't know that right now. Gabe may have told Alex and I'm flying up there tomorrow."

"Well, just in case your dear brother-in-law tries to put the blame for the fire on you, get that information as soon as you can. If nothing else, for your own peace of mind. If the transaction actually took place before either of you were present in the state, then you can probably prove that dear Donald lied when he was questioned by an official investigator. That would turn the spotlight firmly back on him. What a pity you can't undo his election."

Hmm. Maybe we couldn't do that, but this could certainly embarrass him if it got out to his home constituents. It might just be something to hold over his head.

When I got home I called Alex to give him my flight time and pass along Damaris' suggestion.

"Excellent advice; we'll owe her another meal. I didn't think to ask Gabe for that level of detail, but I'll call him and ask him to scan those receipts. I should have them by the time your plane touches down."

CHAPTER NINETEEN
(*Friday, December 6*)

Alex was waiting as soon as I cleared Customs at the Calgary airport. It helped that my husband was slightly famous, certainly among law enforcement personnel, and well-liked. "Welcome home, Mrs. MacLeod," the agent said as he escorted me to the security exit.

"We're having an RCMP meeting over our dinner table tonight." my husband said as he hugged me.

"Am I cooking? If so, what?"

"Stanley is cooking. As the forensics chief he should be leading our meeting, but he assures me he can both walk and whistle. Or at least cook and whistle."

Dr. Stanley Wong was cooking stir-fried shrimp with curried rice. His wife, Staff Sergeant Major Samantha Wong, was making the salad. Our other guests were Rob and Marci Gordon. Rob was head of dispatch at the local RCMP post. He had retired a few years ago after a job-related injury, and then unretired when Marci told him, "I married you for better or for worse, but not for lunch." Marci had been able to wheedle the cheesecake and chocolate mousse recipes from the chef at the Legion and was bringing the dessert tonight.

"Dinner, and a movie," Stanley announced as he served the meal. Alex had run the video feed through the large screen television, as well as a slide show of the still photos of the actual arson scene. We enjoyed our wonderful meal first, and then watched the movie in the living room part of our 'great room,' with dessert and glasses of Scotch or wine.

Stanley watched the presentation critically and then added his comments. "Good work on the part of that young detective for realizing something was wrong," and then he began to tally up the evidence.

"Wait a moment," Alex said, "we don't have our faithful court reporter, and we should write this down."

Marci volunteered, and Stanley began to go through the evidence. "Alex found that there were no functional batteries in any of the smoke detectors in the house. Fingerprints on any of those, Alex?"

"Ahh, we discussed that the first time I was out at the scene but I forgot to ask Gabriel about them when he called. His news startled and distracted me. We do have useful prints from the wine glasses Donald and the chief goon used, and a print on a cocktail glass the other suspect apparently handled."

Stanley continued, "And then you noted that the box of embers that set off the fire was still warm, yet the hearth inside was cold; there had been no fire in their fireplace."

"That's right"

"Then there were the vinyl siding panels stacked on either side of the door from the bedroom to the patio."

"Aye, and that was the news that distracted me. Gabriel had already learned that Jennifer's brother-in-law's credit card paid for those panels. He's a newly elected congressman from the state of Georgia..."

"This information wouldn't reflect to his credit," Stanley commented.

"Absolutely correct," Alex said. "If nothing else this may embarrass him in front of the people who elected him. But there's more; our young detective went back to Atlanta to interview him in relation to that finding. His answer was that his sister-in-law – my wife – asked him to buy them."

"Well, that puts a different face on it," Stanley said. He turned to me. "Did you?"

"Of course not! But there's more; I had planned a new recipe for us while we were there that involved flambéing the chicken in Grand Marnier, but my full bottle had disappeared. When we got back to San Diego I did make that recipe, and almost burned down my kitchen."

"Don't give my wife that recipe," Stanley said. Sam glared at him.

"But after that near-disaster we recalled Dan's arson specialist telling us to look for an accelerant," Alex said, "so we did. There had been a bag of household trash in proximity to the box of hot embers. We asked Gabriel to look into the contents of that bag. He went dumpster-diving and gave us the news that it was mostly paper products, all very flammable, as well as a greasy pizza box. But the cherry on the sundae was an empty bottle of Grand Marnier. Gabriel wasn't confident enough in his own ability to lift prints from a broken and burned bottle, so he asked me to go back over there to assist. The arson expert went with me, and tonight's movie was the result. The print we recovered matched the one on the cocktail glass the under-goon left in our bathroom."

We cleaned our dessert plates, finished our wine and Scotch, and after Sam and Marci washed up and loaded the dishwasher, we said goodnight. We checked on the puppies one more time, gave Belladonna a midnight snack, and went to bed.

We had planned to sleep in, or loll around in bed this morning. But just as Alex's mustache was starting to tickle my ear, the phone rang.

I could hear Stanley's voice as Alex held it away from his ear.

"Alex, you said you were both in Arizona on the day of the fire, but what about the date and time of the actual sale of those siding panels?"

"Good point; Jennifer's friend, the District Attorney, asked her the same thing. We haven't got around to asking Gabe for that information yet; this all came out in just the last two days."

"I suggest you find out as soon as possible; I'm sorry that this is a member of Jennifer's family, but it sounds like he's quickly looking for someone he can shift the blame to. If he tries something like that, phone records can always be retrieved to show whether or not you called him to ask him to do it. We already know he can't claim you made the request in person until you actually arrived there."

Alex looked at his watch. "I'll call Gabriel. They're an hour later than we are; I probably won't get him out of bed."

"Well, I'm sorry about that but you'll want to be ahead of whatever this slimy character tries to do to deflect any blame from himself."

"I'll do that."

"And then call me so we can put our heads together and come up with a plan. I know we have neither jurisdiction nor any real standing, but if he's trying to implicate Jennifer, we should be on the offence. Ask Jennifer if she has a good relationship with the Tucson District Attorney."

"I'll pass the phone to her."

"I heard the question. It's County Attorney there, and I barely know her name. When I gave my deposition to one of the deputies I mentioned Alex's teaching crime scene preservation, and she didn't even recognize his name."

"Is that office likely to be of any help to your detective in charging any of these characters?"

"I just don't have any feeling for how they would handle it."

"Since your own District Attorney is a friend, do you think she'd get involved?"

"We took her to lunch last week," Alex said. "I'm sure she would if she thought she had any influence in Arizona."

"Unfortunately, the attitude in Arizona is that if they do it in California, Arizona won't," I told him.

"Still, it can't hurt to try, even if you're turned down."

"Well, I guess we've got our assignments," I said as I started to get out of bed.

"Not quite so fast, Gabe will still have his phone with him when we're ready to call him."

CHAPTER TWENTY
(*Saturday, December 7*)

Alex made the call while I cooked breakfast. "Gabe, it's Alex MacLeod. Oh, of course you wouldn't have recognized the number; I'm up home in Alberta. Jennifer came up to see our new puppies; over dinner last night we told our friends what was going on down there. Our chief of forensics had an idea and suggested we call you. What is the date and time stamp on Donald's receipt for those vinyl panels?"

"I have those receipts back at my desk; can I call you back at this number?"

"Aye, if we're not here we may be out exercising the horses but leave a message and we'll call you back."

"Horses?"

"Horses. We might try to tempt you up here for a vacation, and fishing on one of the best rivers in Alberta."

"I'm already tempted. I'll be back there about lunch time and call you."

"And even better, scan those receipts to me. Here's the email address."

There wasn't any good reason to sit by the phone all day; if Gabe called he would leave the information for us and send the scanned receipts in an email. We walked down to the barn and bribed our two riding horses with handfuls of sweet feed. The two pack horses, the Baggins, Frodo and Bilbo, got a handful too, but they didn't get haltered and then bridled and saddled. The day was cool – well, coming from Southern California and Tucson – cold, but at least it wasn't threatening snow. By now I knew most of the tricks my part-Arab mare was likely to pull. Fancy, and Alex's gelding, Dusty, had thick winter coats, but that only meant letting out the cinches by one notch, not two. I wasn't tall enough or strong enough to bump a knee into Fancy's belly to make her let out the air she had sucked in, but Alex's knee certainly could. She also found something dangerous and scary along the riverbank that was worth a snort or a buck, no matter how many times that rock hadn't attacked her before.

It was a pleasant ride; we got back to the barn, brushed the horses down and turned them out again, and then went up to the house for lunch.

The answering machine for the house phone was blinking. "Here's a message from Gabriel. He says the receipts are scanned and attached to an email. I'll let him know we've received it."

He opened the email message and downloaded the attached scans. "Aha, lass, here is the evidence of when the vinyl panels were paid for." He downloaded the file and then printed it. "Here's the date, November 2."

"What day of the week was it?"

He went to the wall calendar and turned back a page. "Saturday; when did you get over there?"

"The next Monday. I got there late in the afternoon and there were several phone messages from Donald insisting that I call him."

"When had you last talked to him before that?"

"It was about two weeks; he called me from a fundraising dinner. That date can probably be verified."

"Excellent, so there shouldn't be any records of phone calls between the two of you that he can point to and claim you instructed him to purchase the siding panels."

"For a brick ranch-style house?"

"Or for delivery to the home of your deceased obedience judge."

"Well, what do we do next?"

"We give all of this to Gabriel, with our ideas, and let him run his investigation."

"And then we just sit back and do nothing?"

"Not unless you want to." He hugged me. "We'll stay involved, as long as we don't interfere with Gabriel's investigation, of course."

I had to fly home on Sunday but before I did we went over the puppies again and took pictures of all of them. "When I come back up again in another month we'll be able to make a better evaluation. Among our several litters we'll have to figure out which puppies would be best for our personal breeding programs and those of our friends."

"You'll be back up before the month is up, lass; don't forget the New Year's party."

"Can I get away with one of my old evening gowns?"

"Oh, certainly, unless you want to wear one of your silk nightgowns."

I poked him in the ribs with my elbow, but he was right, it wasn't likely anyone would remember the dress I had worn for my first New Year's up here four years ago.

CHAPTER TWENTY-ONE
(*December 9 –December 10*)

I called Damaris when I got to the office in the morning. She had a vested interest in the case of the dead children in the storage shed since it was our involvement in the case that brought it to the attention of the authorities in the first place.

"Damaris, there's been another development in the Arizona situation and I wonder if you think there's anything you could discuss with your counterpart over there that could move this forward?"

"Does this involve another lunch?"

"By all means; this time we won't need to give Robert another demonstration."

"He'll probably be disappointed. Call Amber, I can be free for lunch tomorrow or Thursday."

Amber was also free and said she'd make our reservations for Tuesday.

Over lunch I reprised Donald's latest devious scheme. "When our friend, the deputy, went back to Atlanta to interview him, Donald claimed that I asked him to order the vinyl siding panels that helped fuel the arson fire. Damaris suggested we get the date and time of the receipts..."

"Jennifer," Damaris broke in, "what you should do now is request a printout from all of your phone providers, covering any calls that could fall within the dates when that could have happened."

"Don't they need a subpoena to release the records?"

"No; I would need a subpoena to get those records, but you have every right to request your own. However, if you run into difficulty, we could consider a subpoena. Just be sure there aren't any calls you wouldn't want made public," she said with a grin.

"Of course not. But are all of our calls recorded?"

"No, all they have are the numbers called from every phone, but those printouts should prove whether or not you and Donald spoke at the time he claims you asked him to purchase those items for you."

"I'll get started on that this afternoon. What about his calls to me?"

"If they're not able to list incoming calls it may be time to enlist the help of your friend in Atlanta."

"Donald also called me several times after he got to the hotel in Tucson."

"But you said the panels were purchased before you arrived there."

"That's right."

"So no problem there, and if anything did look like a problem it would be subpoena time. I think you're covered. What about that other matter over there, the trial of the dude who killed his kids?"

"When I gave my deposition the deputy prosecutor suggested that it would be very convenient for them if Alex and I could make ourselves available during the entire two weeks the trial might take."

"Well, that's asking a bit much, but I could probably negotiate it down to a week for you, which would certainly be paid leave, and we could probably pull that off for Alex as well, although I wouldn't have as much influence on that decision."

"You mean because my husband is Jennifer's boss?" Amber asked.

"Of course; but I'm actually thinking that I can trade some cooperation from the County Attorney in your arson investigation. You or Alex should ask your deputy over there to let us know whatever help he needs to pursue this, and I'll ask the County Attorney to make it happen. I know both of these cases are apparent homicides and equally important, but the case of the kids is so high profile that I think we can use it for leverage."

"Thanks, you're a real friend. If you need to summarize it for her, this started as just the sad death of my obedience judge until we learned that her husband denied a key permit for a development that was important to my brother-in-law's congressional backers. And then the fatal fire that was first investigated and closed as an accident was discovered to be arson. And finally, one of the major flammable components of that fire was apparently stolen from my house, and my cowardly brother-in-law tried to pin the purchase of another on me."

"That sums it up in a few words. Let's have dessert and get to work after we get back to our offices."

When I got back to my office I called the local phone company and after listening to several menus ("Please listen carefully because our options have changed") and several transfers after that, I finally reached a real person who said yes, she could print out phone numbers called from my home landline between October 8 and November 8. "What about incoming calls? Can you also give me numbers that have called my house?" Yes, they could, it might take a little longer. They would be mailed to my billing address. Next I called my cell phone carrier. Donald didn't have that number; we'd requested a new number after my mother wormed it out of a club member when we were in Atlanta just a few months ago, so I didn't need incoming calls from that one. We had a different phone company in Tucson and it was a long distance call from here, but they were an hour later so I could call them from home tomorrow and just come to work a little late if necessary.

My conversation with our Tucson landline carrier was as frustrating as the time I tried to get our pest control company out to the house to deal with a hive of killer bees. I wasn't calling from the number for which I was requesting the records. "That's because I'm not there right now. I'm at my other home in San Diego."

"Well, we can only take such a request for the records of that number when it's called in from that number. You can mail a request to us and we can mail the report back to the service address."

"I wanted the information sooner than that; I guess I could fly over there for the weekend."

"Our office hours are Monday through Friday, eight AM to five PM."

Well, shit! I could probably ask our nearest neighbors to make the call and the request from the house, but I hated to involve them in Donald's sordid plot. I stewed about it for the rest of the day until I went home and called Alex.

"Well, lass, I think your friends are right that we should be forearmed with this information before he ever tries to bring it up in case of a criminal investigation."

"Then I guess I'd better fly over Sunday and make my calls Monday morning."

"I can probably find a student to stay over the weekend if you want me to join you there."

"I'd love to have you there, but it's not really necessary. I'll fly over Sunday, make the calls Monday, and then fly back home."

CHAPTER TWENTY-TWO
(*December 15 – December 16*)

It was almost the shortest day of the year and it was dark by the time the airport shuttle dropped me off at the house. Our neighbor, Augie, had turned on the outdoor spots and the porch light so I could find my way to the front door. I was the last drop-off and the driver waited with his headlights aimed at the door until I opened it. For some reason the key didn't turn as smoothly as it should have. I turned on lights as I went through the house to the master bedroom to drop off my small carry-on and then to the kitchen to dig something simple out of the freezer. I had just pulled out a catfish filet when the phone rang. It was early for Alex to call; it was never certain that my plane would land on time or that I would get home this quickly. The caller ID showed a local, familiar number. When I picked it up a voice asked, "Jennifer, is that you?"

"Yes, of course."

"There was someone there at your front door yesterday. He was trying to force open the door. I called 911 first, and then walked over with my little snake gun. The guy said he had been here last month and left something important inside. I told him I didn't think that gave him a right to break into the house. I was glad I had taken the little gun because he told me I should mind my own business, so I told him I would, just as soon as the sheriff arrived so he decided to not wait around that long."

"Augie, thank you so much. Did the sheriff show up?"

"Yes, and it was your friend, Deputy Moreno. He told me there had been some unsavory characters that he helped remove from your house. He gave me a number that would always reach him and not the dispatch."

"He was right, Augie, there were a couple of really nasty guys that my brother-in-law allowed in our home. You really shouldn't try to confront any of them on our behalf, just call Gabriel's number and let them handle it. They scared me when they were here in my house."

"So is there something of his in your house?"

"Not that I know of, I came over so I could call the phone company here in the morning, and then I'm going back to San Diego again the same morning. If there's anything that bothers you when we're not here, call the sheriff, and call us, but don't get in the way of someone who might be violent."

"I won't, Jennifer, but you are good neighbors and we have to look out for you."

We would have to get nice Christmas gifts for Augie, his wife, Dominique, and their daughter, Tiffany.

While the catfish thawed I called Alex. His phone went to voice mail and I left a message. "Alex, I'm here in Tucson and Augie said there was someone here yesterday trying to get into the house. I don't have copies of our mug shots from last month; can you email them to me here so I can show them to Augie?" He was probably down at the barn feeding the horses. I went around the house checking that doors and windows were locked. My catfish filet was simmering in butter when Alex called me back.

"Jennifer, lass, I wish I had come down to go over there with you. Maybe you should go to a hotel for tonight and then make your call from the house in the morning."

"No, that's silly; he probably won't come back and try to find his way inside after dark through all the cactus, and I already made sure everything was locked up tight. I wish I had your head on the other pillow, or even Monty's, but it's just overnight, I'll keep my cell phone on the nightstand, and my flight back is late morning after I request the phone records."

"In addition to your cell phone, get our snake gun out of the dining room hutch and put it in the nightstand."

"Will that be of any use against an intruder?"

"If you have to use it, aim for his face. And call me first thing in the morning so I can be assured that you made it safely through the night. Oh, and call Gabriel to let him know you're there."

"Good idea, and maybe he can get his hands on those mug shots."

"But I'll send them anyway. We should find out if Augie saw one of them. I have them here at home and I'll send them now."

I turned on the computer in the room we used as an office and then looked for a veg to have with my catfish. Frozen green peas in a cream sauce was one of my very few options so I poured a serving of them into a microwave dish and thawed them.

I called Gabriel and told him I was here at the house, downloaded the mug shots Alex had emailed, called Augie and then emailed them to him.

Gabriel told me to call him anytime, no matter what time of night; Augie said, yes, the man trying to force my front door looked very much like the tough under-goon Donald had brought to the house. When I finally went to bed it took me a long time to fall asleep, and once I did, something must have stimulated my subconscious because I woke up with a start, remembering that Alex had told me to tuck the snake gun into the nightstand.

I turned over a couple of times and then decided that I wasn't going to fall asleep again until I did what Alex had suggested. I turned on the light, found my slippers, and walked to the dining room. The gun was in the middle drawer of the hutch, I took it out, checked that it was loaded, and brought it back to the bedroom.

I opened the nightstand drawer and started to put it in, and then noticed something out of place. There shouldn't have been anything in that drawer except a couple of my nightgowns and an emergency flashlight, but there was a large, fat brown envelope that had been shoved in there under my nightgowns. I pulled it out and closed the drawer, leaving the gun on top of the nightstand. If someone got into the house during the night I didn't want to have to open a drawer to fumble for the gun. I hoped I could remember which way the safety worked, and that I'd be able to aim it accurately.

In the morning no one had broken in during the night and after I showered I called Alex to tell him so. "I'm relieved, lass, but still concerned about the attempt. Call me again when you're at the airport."

"I will, and there was something here that might have been behind that attempt." I told him about the envelope in the nightstand.

"What's in it?"

"I haven't looked yet, but it looked like it was shoved in there quickly. The only time that could have happened was when Donald decided to hide out in our bedroom and he didn't want anyone to look at it when we went in there to smoke him out."

He snorted. "Probably not your best choice of words, lass, but I get the point. You may as well investigate the contents, and then take it back home with you."

"I will, I'll go through it on the plane."

I made a quick breakfast of scrambled eggs, and promptly at eight o'clock I called our local phone provider. It still took several transfers and quite a bit of time on hold, but I finally talked to someone who seemed to have the authority to make it happen. "I hope you can send these records to me quickly; there's possibly a legal case involved here, and if necessary we'll get a subpoena."

"Oh, that shouldn't be necessary; the report should be mailed to your billing address within the week."

Augie's daughter collected our mail when we weren't there and her parents sorted it to forward anything important. I could count on them to send the phone records as soon as they were received. With the whole purpose of my quick trip accomplished, I called for an airport shuttle. When it beeped outside I grabbed my overnight bag and locked the front door as I left. As I did I felt another chill; there were marks next to the lock where the white paint had been scraped down to the raw metal. It looked like someone had tried to pry the door open. So that was why the key hadn't turned as smoothly as I remembered.

I called Alex when I arrived at the airport, but decided to wait to tell him about the door until I got back home. I had an hour-long wait to clear security and another hour in the air to look through the contents of the envelope. No wonder Donald had tried to hide it when we went looking for him. There were printouts of emails, and transcripts of apparently recorded or eavesdropped phone calls. It was an ugly chronology; all of the correspondence seemed to have involved Donald, either to him or from him, or somehow obtained by him. There were emails more or less ordering Donald to call someone, or be somewhere for a meeting, and then ordering him to Arizona to, "Take care of that Fish guy." Other memos covered meetings between some high-level Washington persons and people who seemed to be 'influencers' and finally newspaper clippings that cited several trips by a Cabinet member to the private lodge and hunting preserve of the wealthy developer who wanted to build the Benson monstrosity, followed by messages from someone to Donald that, "The Secretary wants this DONE. If you don't want to find yourself on a back bench in Congress, see to it!"

There was much more to be gone through as we got the announcement to put away our trays and return our seats to the upright position. I tucked it all back into the envelope and slid it into the side pocket of my carry-on. I'd have to study the material more thoroughly, and this looked like something I should share with my good friends and legal consultants over another lunch. But it was almost Christmas and I was flying north on Friday to spend Christmas and New Year's with Alex. I'd call Damaris and Amber when I got home, and use the rest of today to copy all of the contents of the envelope for them.

I paid Mandy, generously, for house-sitting over the weekend. "What do you think of the puppies?"

"Oh my God, they're gorgeous."

"Well, I've put together all the pedigrees of all of the litters we're expecting all around our country and Canada. We get a puppy back from your Brewster and BonBon, and if you like we can make another trade if someone else in this circle is interested in one of your litter."

"Oh, neat! I want to start another puppy, but it doesn't make sense to keep one from my own litter."

"Take this stack of pedigrees home and see what looks like it will work for you."

It was still early enough to call Damaris and Amber and try to arrange a lunch date this week. They were both in court this afternoon so I left messages asking them to call. "There's been a new twist in the Arizona problem and you'll want to hear about it. I just flew back from there and I have some interesting documents to show you. Call me at home and let's set up a lunch."

Damaris called a little after five o'clock. "You sure aroused our curiosity, girl. I called Amber and we're both free for lunch Wednesday. Amber says that's her husband's managers' meeting, so meet us downtown when it's over. I'll make the reservations. And by the way, Clarke Davidson is getting a little bored in retirement; would you mind if we invite him?"

"Of course I don't mind. He should find this really interesting and convoluted. Even if none of our players have jurisdiction, we're still up to our ears in it."

"Or up to your rears in it," Damaris joked. "See you Wednesday."

I had scanned the whole wretched packet into my computer and made two sets of copies for Damaris and Amber; now it looked like I needed another for Judge Davidson. While I was at it, I may as well make a couple of copies to take to Canada this weekend.

I opened another package of paper for the printer and while I was loading it the phone on the desk rang. I answered it without checking the display and heard my brother-in-law-s voice. "Jennifer, I forgot a very important package at your house last month. I need you to mail me the key. Overnight express. Right away."

"And a very good evening to you too, Donald. How did you happen to forget something so important?"

"It slipped my mind when your people were so rudely forcing me out of the house."

"Donald, I've told you over and over again that I'm not mailing a key to you or anyone connected to you."

"Then mail it to your neighbor and he can let me in."

"The same neighbor who ran off one of your goons last week? The goon he said was trying to break into my house?"

"What? Were you at the house? If you were, why didn't you answer the door? I left messages saying I needed that material."

There hadn't been any messages on the Tucson phone, but knowing Donald, he probably just figured breaking into the house was easier than asking me for whatever he forgot. I was thankful our security doors had thwarted the attempt.

"I got there the day after the attempted break-in. Once again the answer is no. I'm not mailing a key to you, or to a neighbor, or anyone else, and I'd like to know why you tried to hide those papers in my bedroom." Donald had no need to know that our neighbors already had a key.

"WHAT? Jennifer, those are confidential papers; you have no right to have your hands on them!"

"I have every right to investigate anything I find in my house. And speaking of rights, what right did you have to claim that I asked you to buy one of the components of a fatal arson fire?"

"I can't be involved in a scandal if someone committed arson. I can't have any damage to my reputation while I'm waiting to be seated in Congress. It could hurt my chances of a committee appointment."

"But you lied, and tried to damage my reputation."

"Well, you'll think of some reason why you needed them. You'd better work on it; my reputation is much more important. Meanwhile, I need those papers back right away. Where are they? This is a matter of national security, dammit! Do you have them with you in San Diego? If so, I'll fly someone out there tonight to get them from you."

I definitely didn't want one of Donald's goons showing up here at my door. "No, I left them in Tucson in my safe deposit box." I told that lie with a straight face that would probably have convinced Donald even if he had been looking right at me. Even Alex might admit that I could manage a poker face when it counted. Meanwhile, I'd finish making my copies tonight, and before I went to the office in the morning I planned to stop at my credit union here and put the originals in the safe deposit box. It might also be a good idea to take the copies for the DA, the judge and the public defender to the office with me since I'd be going to our lunch from there. One more bit of insurance might be to lodge the copies I was taking to Canada with Marcus across the street until he took me to the airport on Friday. I had long ago stopped thinking of my eightyish neighbor as a frail, elderly man since he regularly went to the shooting range to stay qualified, didn't hesitate to stay in my house to protect me, and usually came armed.

Donald was still nattering at the other end of the line when I hung up the phone and sent a command to the printer. When I had all of the copies I needed I put each set in a large envelope and stuck a sticky note on each one with the name of the intended recipient. I called Alex to fill him in on this latest wrinkle.

"Jennifer, lass, this worries me even more than the attempt to break into the Tucson house. Have you told Dan?"

"No, I just now hung up on Donald while he was still talking."

"Call him now, and call Marcus. Maybe it would be a good idea to ask Marcus to spend some time in the house while you're at work. If someone did break in, some harm could come to the puppies."

"Oh God, I didn't think of that. When Donald's goon was shoving me out of our own house Monty growled at him and he threatened to break his neck. Yes, it would be a good idea to have someone here until I take the dogs to Bonnie Thursday."

After we said good night I called Dan's cell. He picked up on the second ring.

"Jennifer? I'm at Bonnie's, what's up?"

I filled him in. "I haven't even read all the files thoroughly yet, but there seems to be almost proof of guilt running through them. If it was worth killing the Fish and Wildlife supervisor for the permit, it looks like these papers that tend to prove it would also be worth killing for. When Donald said he'd fly someone out here to get them from me I told him they were in my safe deposit box in Tucson, but he might still send someone to twist my arm to get them for him."

"Alex had a good idea. Call Marcus and ask him to check on your house several times over the next few days, I'll make a point of driving by when I can...wait a minute. What, Bonnie?"

Bonnie took the phone from him. "Jen, bring Misty and the puppies here tomorrow. You probably want to keep the boys there until you leave, but the puppies are too helpless to risk if someone wants to break into your house."

"You're right. I have to go to the credit union in El Cajon to put the originals in the safe deposit box. I'll take them to you first."

Dan took the phone back. "Make another set of copies to leave with Bonnie. I'll go through them too. Maybe I'll have more good ideas."

I told him that Alex had advised me to put the snake gun in the nightstand, which led to my discovery of the files.

"Another excellent idea. Do you have a gun in the house here?"

"No, although he's threatened to teach me about firearms."

"It's time to take him up on it. You don't have to become a gun collector or hoarder, but given the number of villains you seem to attract, you should know how to use one."

I called Marcus next and he agreed with everything Alex and Dan had said. He volunteered to come now and stay the night.

"No, even if Donald was able to get someone on a plane tonight he couldn't arrive before sometime tomorrow. But I'll be very grateful to have someone guarding the house for the next few days."

"I'll take my salary in dinners."

I felt much safer now. I fed the dogs, made my own dinner, and finally went to bed with Monty's head on the next pillow.

CHAPTER TWENTY-THREE
(*Wednesday, December 18*)

I had delivered Misty and the puppies to Bonnie, and the originals of Donald's files to my safe deposit box Tuesday morning; now I was looking forward to lunch with my good friends in law and order.

We met for lunch after Wendell's last manager's meeting of the year. Robert, the *maître d'*, had set up our table in the private dining room. When Judge Davidson joined us, Robert brought our menus, and then told Judge Davidson that he had seen the video of the reenactment of the arson fire and it had been very impressive.

"And I have also seen the results of that liqueur in a flambé gone wrong, right here in this kitchen. I can well believe it started a fatal fire." He had a sly smile on his face when he told us, "I could arrange a special lunch if anyone needs convincing."

"Maybe a flambé specialty for one of these meetings," Judge Davidson said.

"With a day's advance notice, we can make that possible," Robert told him. "Would you like to order now?"

"What is today's dessert?" Amber asked.

"A chocolate mousse with whipped cream and fresh raspberries."

Amber and Damaris ordered salads, I ordered today's quiche, and we all looked forward to dessert.

Judge Davidson skimmed the packet of papers and memos while we waited for our food. "Jennifer, this is extremely troubling. Whether or not it's evidence of murder, it is evidence of official corruption at very high levels, undue influence on an elected member of Congress and attempting to pressure an official of a government agency for personal gain."

Amber and Damaris had been reading their own packets. "I totally concur," Damaris told me. She added, "It looks like there might be enough evidence to arrest any of them who could be lured to Arizona. Can you do that?"

"Not during the next couple of weeks. I'm spending Christmas and New Year's in Canada, and we don't have any reason to visit Tucson in the near future."

"What about the trial of the children's killer?" Damaris asked. "If you go over for that you'd have a perfect reason to tell Donald to meet you there to retrieve his property."

"We haven't heard anything from the County Attorney since we gave our depositions."

"Let me see what I can find out," Damaris said. "If there's the possibility of a trial date we can use that as your reason for being there. If there isn't a date," with a sly chuckle, "we can just stretch the truth a little and tell them you're in town for the case."

CHAPTER TWENTY-FOUR
(*December 20 – December 21*)

Misty and her puppies had been safely tucked away with Bonnie since the morning after Donald's disturbing phone call. Yesterday after work I delivered Dragon to the kennel. Marcus Todd had suggested a brilliant solution to my worry about being alone last night without even a dog in the house.

"Monty knows me well enough after all these years, and he certainly knows Rosebud and Poppy. Keep him home with you tonight and bring him over to my house when I take you to the airport in the morning."

"Do you really want three dogs for the next couple of weeks?"

"Two haven't been a problem, and anyway, Rosebud really only sleeps all day. She wakes up for meals; that's how I can tell she's still alive"

I had taken several still photos of each puppy and a few short videos to bring with me. After Dragon's brilliant debut as a herding dog when he had helped save me from a flock of stampeding sheep, we had planned our two litters with the ranchers of Alberta in mind. Alex had placed his Champion Abercoul Tobermory – Toby – with the sheep rancher Ralph Denny, who had adopted my retired bitch, Angel, several years ago.

Laura and Eric Sutton were the cattle ranchers who had introduced the first herding Cardigan to the area, Champion Brookside Nightshade, Toby's sire as well as litter brother to Alex's beloved Belladonna. During our recent holiday that included herding trials on both sides of our border, the Suttons and Ralph Denny had expressed interest in bitch puppies to eventually raise more herding dogs.

With all the other litters of interest to us across both countries we should be able to satisfy everyone with outstanding puppies.

Alex's litter was over a week younger than mine. Belladonna had been bred to Toby; those puppies and my Dragon-Misty litter were the pups we thought had the best potential of becoming working stock dogs. Since my own focus was toward show ring wins and obedience titles, I hoped some of these puppies that went to working homes might also be shown.

Alex met me at the airport in Calgary and drove us south to our home in Lethbridge. "No dinner guests tonight, lass, but I did invite our friends for tomorrow night. Laura and Eric want to come look at the puppies tomorrow, and Ralph and Lois would also like to visit, but he doesn't want to impose on us just before Christmas, and he said after working with Dragon and then seeing how he used that training to help move the sheep that were charging at you, he's inclined to favor a pup from your litter."

"Well that makes sense; his dog is the sire of your pups, after all."

"And the more genetic diversity we can bring to the area, the better. Did you bring up puppy pictures?"

"I emailed them to us at the house, and I have a disk with some video. When did Ralph want to visit?"

"Whenever you say it's convenient."

"Let's call him tonight; we owe him a puppy after he trained Dragon so well."

"Aye, and I'm eternally grateful to him for that. You call him when we get to the house."

I did, and thanked him again for training Dragon well enough that he could help turn the stampede of sheep that was supposed to push me, and the Montana rancher's young son, over a cliff and into a raging river. "I have photos and video of Dragon's litter, and Alex said you'd like to visit these puppies."

"We would, but we don't want to interfere with your Christmas holiday."

"You won't be interfering; Laura and Eric are planning to pay us a visit tomorrow, you and Lois are welcome whenever you can drive down here."

"Well, maybe we'll go down there tomorrow so you can get rid of us all at once."

"You're welcome to stay for supper; Alex informed me that we're feeding a few of our RCMP friends. Whatever we cook will stretch, and Alex's dinner table will easily seat a dozen or more."

"Oh, no, we won't stay for supper, but we'd like to see you

again, and Lois is absolutely silly over the prospect of playing with puppies."

"Then as long as you don't show up before breakfast, come ahead. If nothing else I'll have a pasta salad for lunch."

"I remember your last one; we may take you up on that."

Alex mixed up the dinner bowls for Arwen and Luna while I made Belladonna's dinner and brought it to her. I served it in the whelping box, and the puppies crowded around the dish. Belladonna growled at them so I moved the dish out of the box.

"Alex, it's time to mix up a dish for the puppies; they wanted to investigate their mother's dinner."

"I'll let you take charge of that tomorrow; you've had far more experience."

He grilled elk steaks that had marinated in red wine almost since I made my flight reservations. Elk was more tender than venison since they were grazing rather than browsing animals, but still, wild game needed tenderizing. His walk-in freezer had several packages of pre-cooked, stuffed baked potatoes; I popped a couple of those into one of the ovens and then started a pot of water on the stove to boil pasta for tomorrow's lunch. I might as well make enough for a crowd; it would eventually all be eaten.

Alex had fed the horses and put them in their stalls before he went to pick me up so all we had to do before we went to bed ourselves was to tuck in all the dogs.

Sunday morning Alex made pancakes for breakfast while I made up the large pasta salad for lunch. Elbow macaroni, chopped celery and onion, dill relish, chopped hard-boiled eggs, and a mayonnaise dressing. I rummaged around in the freezer shelves and found a bag of tiny frozen shrimp. I dropped a couple of generous handfuls of those in boiling water for a few minutes and then mixed them into the salad. This would feed our puppy visitors very well.

With that finished I started on a meal for the puppies. Alex had been feeding Belladonna puppy chow, as many of our veterinarians had been recommending for some years. He now had a blender – since I had bought it for us a year or so ago. I filled the blender about half-full of kibble, added milk to raise it by another third, and then added a couple of generous scoops of canned dog food. The resulting slurry went into a pie plate – I had bought those for our kitchen too – and I served the plate to the puppies after Alex took their mother out for a walk. The puppies were comical: they didn't know what it was, but they shuffled their way into the dish – and through it. They ate some of it and walked through more of it until they were well coated in puppy meal. When Alex brought their mother back in she washed them – gaining another meal of her own in the process. It was what I usually considered a successful first introduction of puppies to soft food.

Alex had some doubts. "They don't look very presentable for puppy buyers, lass."

"Don't worry, Belladonna will have them presentable by the time our guests have finished the pasta salad."

Our guests wanted to see puppies even before they had lunch, but Belladonna had cleaned them up pretty well. I checked them over before everyone arrived and wiped down a couple of them with a damp washcloth. The puppies weren't very active or amusing at this age, but they were round and furry and cute. Laura and Eric would take one of this litter, but Ralph Denny still wanted one of Dragon's daughters. I had recorded short videos so I brought out the disk to play on Alex's computer. Ralph and Lois watched that with us while Laura and Eric stayed at the whelping box to pick up and cuddle puppies.

"How can you, or anyone, tell which of those bitch puppies is the best candidate for a job as a herding dog?" Ralph asked.

"I don't know, but I do know people who do it with their own dogs and they may be able to give me some tips."

Alex volunteered, "We'll bring the two you like best up here for you to take your choice. I'll keep the other one."

I added, "If the pup doesn't work out for the job you picked her for, I always promise to take her back and replace her."

"Oh, no." Lois said, "If the puppy grows up with us, she'll always have a home."

My kind of people. "With Ralph as a trainer she can't help but be good. Look at what he did with Dragon who had never seen sheep before."

Laura was interested in the brindle female, or the sable that looked like their mother, Belladonna. "I don't want to make my choice based on color, but all other things being equal, what could we expect from either of them bred to Shadow?"

"You mean what color would their puppies be?"

"Yes, not that it matters, but I'm curious."

"I think you could get any or all of their colors with either the brindle or the sable. The other one with Toby's coloring would give you a whole litter of only black and white with brindle points."

"Well, I don't want to make the decision based on color, but it's nice to know what we could expect."

We had our lunch at Alex's huge table, still talking about puppies. Laura would make her choice between her two favorite puppies after a few more weeks and as soon as my litter was old enough I'd bring up the two puppies Lois and Ralph preferred.

Our puppy visitors left with pictures and video of their own, plus copies of what I had brought up with me.

"What am I going to cook for our law and order dinner guests?"

"Given the focus of our deliberations, I thought we should start with a flambé. I laid in all of the ingredients for your zucchini canoes. You can showcase a southwest recipe, as well as give a demonstration of arson by flambé."

"You want us to burn down this kitchen?"

"Noo, but we can give a good preview to your documents and maybe replay the movie."

It was an impressive start to the evening even though the tequila used in this recipe wasn't quite as volatile as the Grand Marnier in the last one.

"You set the scene nicely," Stanley told me, "we're only missing eerie music and a blizzard raging outside."

While our dinner finished cooking Rob and Samantha studied the packets I had brought up, the copies of Donald's mysterious, important files that he had tried to hide under my nightgowns.

"This is pure corruption!" Sam exclaimed. "These memos clearly suggest that your Fish and Wildlife supervisor was told, more than once, that if he didn't approve the permit for that monstrosity of a housing project, that his career was finished."

Rob added his opinion. "Here's evidence that the official who was putting pressure on your brother-in-law took at least a couple of all-expense trips – at government expense – to the developer's private ranch and hunting preserve."

Stanley, the forensic expert, was examining another set of documents; printouts of emails between what sounded like a staffer of the Cabinet member and Donald that made the position blatantly clear. "Donny, boy, we got you this election, now it's payoff time. We expect you to come through. You said you had a relative with a house down there. Get access to it for a secure meeting with some of my people. That permit must be approved no matter what it takes. My people will give you instructions when they meet with you. I repeat – GET IT DONE!"

"Getting it done apparently included murder if all else failed," Stanley observed. "I'd like to see your video again, and the photos of the crime scene. I don't suppose you made a video of your own kitchen fire, did you?"

"Noo, we hadn't actually been expecting that, but when Gabriel found what was probably Jennifer's missing bottle of Grand Marnier it made the connection pretty clear."

"Well, I think your deputy has sufficient grounds for an arrest."

"When I had lunch with our District Attorney and a Public Defender a couple of days ago they suggested that I lure Donald back to Tucson so he could be arrested there."

"My objection to their plan is that if he brought some of his 'people' along it would put Jennifer within reach of them after her brother-in-law didn't bother to protect her from one of those same people, in her own home."

"Yes, but it could work if you and Gabriel were there to arrest Donald. I wouldn't have to be out of your sight for even a minute, and frankly, I don't see cowardly Donald overpowering me. What could go wrong?"

"Don't say that! Don't even think it. In Arizona it's almost certain that if those goons accompany Donald, they'll be armed, and even with Gabriel as backup, I don't want to end up in a gunfight with you as the prize."

"What if we joined you?" Stanley asked.

Samantha looked up, startled. "Really? Not that I mind, of course, I'd love another go at the souvenir shops in Tombstone. But how are we going to arrange it, and can we get official authorization?"

"We can get first class tickets for you to come down on holiday if we can't come up with any better reason," I told them. "I'd feel a lot better about trying that scheme with two more of you at my back, and maybe it could work."

"It sounds like your brother-in-law is cowardly enough that any of us could take him down with no trouble, but if he brings reinforcements, we'll be more than a match for them."

"Unfortunately, he'll already be confirmed as a member of Congress by the time we can get back down there to try to set anything up. The new session of Congress starts while I'm still up here. We just plain ran out of time to do anything about it."

"It might put a crimp in his new career if he's arrested," Sam pointed out. "He might even have to resign."

"That would be sweet," I said, "but until I can get back down there again, let's enjoy our holiday season."

Calabasas Rellenos

When your neighbor down the street leaves a bushel of zucchini on your porch in the dead of night, this is the recipe for you! Start with a zucchini the size of a small canoe, slice lengthwise, cut off ends and parboil until tender. Scrape out seeds and pulp and set aside. One large zucchini half or two small ones per person.

1 pound ground beef

1 medium onion, chopped

1 tsp chopped serrano pepper

1 cup shredded Gouda or Swiss cheese

1 diced tomato

Generous splash of tequila to flambé

2 Tbsp. salsa to taste

Oil for cooking

Salt & pepper

Sour cream

Sauté beef in oil, add onion, tomato and Serrano. When beef is browned pour in tequila and toss in a lighted match. Have fire extinguisher handy. When flames subside remove match, add salsa and adjust seasoning. Spoon meat mixture into zucchini boats, top with sour cream and cheese. A chilled half avocado filled with Italian dressing makes a nice accompaniment. Serves four.

CHAPTER TWENTY-FIVE
(January 1 – January 2)

It had been a lovely holiday time up north and I flew home on an almost empty flight while almost everyone else was either nursing hangovers, or watching football games – or both. Marcus met me at the airport with the motor home, and a surprise passenger. Monty had ridden with him and jumped up on my legs when I got in.

"I thought you'd be glad to see him; he's certainly glad to see you, although he didn't sulk when I fed him and handed out treats."

"I hope he wasn't a problem."

"Not at all, and Poppy was happy to have company; Rosebud sleeps most of the day, although she does wake up for her meals. As long as she still enjoys something in life I'm not really worried."

He had turned on a few lights in the house and when I let us in he went around the house checking doors and windows, and looked into every room, even the closets. "I'm sure if anyone was hiding in here Monty would have sniffed him out by now, but now we can both be comfortable that you're safe tonight."

When I called Marcus with my flight time I asked him to take a ground beef out of the freezer before he picked me up. I put together a meatloaf with two rows of large stuffed olives between layers of ground beef, topped with a good Italian sauce, and finally, strips of bacon in a lattice design over the top.

Marcus reported that he had seen no attempts to break into the house while I was gone. But when I went into my home office to turn on the computer, the answering machine was blinking furiously. The display showed twelve messages, roughly one a day since I had flown to Canada, the most recent earlier today. "Goddammit, Jennifer, where in the hell are you? I've left messages at both of your houses. I warn you. I'm running out of patience. Those files you're holding illegally concern national security. If you don't return them to me right away, I'll have you arrested!"

That last message was from a totally unfamiliar number and area code. I looked it up online and it was in Washington, DC. I opened the computer file of Donald's documents and sent it to the printer.

"Marcus, it looks like my brother-in-law finally made it to Washington. These are the papers I didn't have time to show you before I left, but take a look at this copy while dinner is baking."

Marcus was reading the pages while we each sipped a glass of red wine. "Jennifer, I'm not a lawyer, but I sure sat through enough hearings to recognize that this sounds like a conspiracy to commit a murder."

"Damaris and Amber thought I should lure him back to Tucson so Gabriel could arrest him, and maybe catch a couple of his goons at the same time."

"I sincerely hope you're not thinking of doing anything that risky."

"I wouldn't with only yourg Gabriel as my backup, but naturally Alex would be there, and we had two more volunteers when I was up north. You met RCMP officer Samantha Wong and her husband at Sabrina and Jerry's wedding. With four such capable defenders we should be able to pull it off."

"Well, that sounds a lot safer, but I still don't like the idea of you being set up as bait."

"You make it sound like I'll be tied out like a goat."

"Well, I hope they have a better plan than that but it still makes me nervous."

"I don't think there's a plan yet, it will take a lot more plotting, and anyway, with Donald in Washington now, it may be hard to get him there."

That was apparently the cue for the oven timer to start beeping and the phone to ring. "I'll get the phone, Marcus; will you just turn off the timer? I'll check our dinner after I get off the phone." I was expecting Alex and didn't check the display.

"Goddammit, Jennifer, it's about time you answered your phone! Where are my documents? I want to know where they are, and I'll send one of my people to collect them."

"Good evening, and a Happy New Year to you too, Donald."

"Cut out your bullshit! Where are my papers?"

"Donald, I just got home from Canada, the oven timer just went off to say our dinner is ready, and I want to sit down to eat. This isn't a good time."

"Don't you try to put me off! I've been calling you for two weeks."

"What a shame; I was with my husband for the holidays. Those documents are in my safe deposit box in Tucson. When I go back to Tucson, I can scan them and email them to you."

"Don't you dare! Don't you dare open that packet; all of that material is highly confidential."

"Not to worry, Donald, I know you've never paid attention to my career, but I handle confidential matters every day. Is this a good number to reach you when I'm back in Tucson?"

Maybe not, I heard a string of profanity, and I hung up the phone.

The phone had been on speaker and Marcus heard every word of that exchange. "Jennifer, he's really making me nervous. If you go over to Tucson to lure him, would you like me to go over with you?"

"Thanks, but if Stanley and Sam come down to take part in this sting, they'll have our guest room."

"I can afford a hotel room."

"Of course you can, but we might need some of our troops back here. I wouldn't put it past him to have someone try to break in here. I wonder if it's safe to bring Misty and the pups back here."

"If you do, I'll keep a close eye on the house, or even stay over here and watch your television instead of my own."

"That makes me feel better. I'll bring them home after work tomorrow."

I pulled the meatloaf out of the oven and checked it for doneness. It needed more time, and I needed to boil egg noodles to go with it. I started a pan of water and asked Marcus to let me know when it came to a boil. "I'll call Alex; he may have tried while Donald was ranting at me."

Alex had been trying, and while he wasn't pleased at Donald's continued harassment, he thought it looked promising for their scheme to lure Donald to Tucson in order to arrest him. "Of course you're just back from holiday so you'll have to see how things are going at your office, but ask Madame District Attorney if there's been any progress on a court date for the child killer. That would give you an official reason for being there. I'll ask Sam and Stanley to check on whether or not they can take a holiday on very short notice."

"I'll invite our friends to another lunch when I go back to work tomorrow."

Marcus had brought over my accumulated mail, which included the printout of our Arizona telephone records. Before I went to bed I scanned them into the computer and emailed copies to Alex in Alberta and to our house in Tucson.

In the morning there was nothing resembling a crisis at my office so I called Damaris. "Madame District Attorney, I'm back from Canada with a full-blown plot cooked up by my husband. It's worth another lunch if you're free."

She called back later in the morning. "It's still a slow week for crime; I called Amber and she's free tomorrow, or almost any day next week. I suggest next week so I can call the Pima County Attorney."

"I'll be waiting for your call."

CHAPTER TWENTY-SIX
(January 7 – January 9)

Damaris called me mid-morning. "The Pima County Attorney's office would love to go to court, but the other side insists they need an indefinite continuance, that they can't go forward with their defense until they can bring the father's girlfriend as their chief witness. They contend that she was actually the one who starved the kids to death."

"And Daddy didn't notice?"

"Apparently since he wasn't familiar with small children, he left it all to her. He said she withheld food when they misbehaved."

"How badly can two preschool children misbehave in order to be starved to death?"

"Exactly. So defense counsel insists that the girlfriend has to be present to testify, and the girlfriend is believed to be somewhere in Mexico."

"And of course the defense will be quick to accuse the girlfriend of the actual murder, so of course she's not going to be easy to find and extradite."

"You got it. So there goes your excuse to be in Tucson. Amber and I are both free for lunch tomorrow; meet us at the restaurant and we'll try to figure out an alternate reason for you to be there. How much notice does your husband need?"

"Not as much as our other friends might need. I'll tell you all about that over lunch."

Over another outstanding meal I told them of Sam and Stanley's offer to join us in Tucson for the arrest. "I wasn't keen on being tied out like a sacrificial goat with only Alex and Gabriel to defend me, possibly outnumbered by Donald's goons, but with those two also guarding my back, the odds are more on our side."

"Who are they again?"

"You may remember them from Sabrina's wedding. Staff Sargent-Major Samantha Wong, RCMP: she's the officer who tackled

Bob Voczek and sat on him while Sabrina's husband put the handcuffs on him. Dr. Stanley Wong, her husband, is chief of forensics – he also teaches at the University – and while not as good a tackle as his wife, he could probably handle cowardly Donald."

"In that case, let's concoct a reason for you to be in Tucson."

"How about a dog show?" Amber asked.

"None in January."

"A problem with the house?" Damaris asked. "A blown water line?"

"Maybe, or maybe, just friends coming down for a Southern Arizona vacation so he can meet us while we're there with our friends."

"That may be your best idea; when in doubt, tell the truth as much as possible," Amber said.

"Excellent advice from a Public Defender," Damaris told her with a grin. "I'll keep that in mind next time I'm up against you in court."

"Well, we know I won't have to defend Jennifer, but wouldn't you love to be the one to prosecute her brother-in-law and his friends?"

"Oh, yes! It would be a real step up to prosecute a Congressman when my highest profile so far is a politician who didn't quite win an election for mayor."

"We could probably make a real party of it if you two want to join us; Marcus Todd already volunteered."

"We'd certainly make quite a posse."

"We'd probably just be in the way," Amber said, "but be sure you let us know when it's going to happen."

"And be sure to take video if you can," Damaris added.

"I'm not sure about that, but we will if there's any way possible."

When I got home that evening I called Alex. "Our friends approve of the plan, so whenever Sam and Stanley can get away, let's set it up."

"I'll call them now."

He called me back Thursday after work. "Sam and Stanley are thrilled at the prospect of helping us arrest another villain. They can get away with a week's notice so Sam suggested they fly down to Tucson a week from today. I can get a flight that arrives Wednesday so we can drive over then."

"I'll call Donald and tell him I'll be available to meet with him next Friday."

Donald's time zone was three hours later than mine so I fed the dogs and then thawed and sautéed a salmon filet that I ate with steamed broccoli and Hollandaise sauce. After the dogs had spent enough time in the yard, and I had watched the most interesting segments of the evening news, I called the number I had written down after Donald's last telephone rant.

The sleepy voice that answered made me smile, but I carefully kept it out of my own voice.

"Um, hullo, who's this?"

"Donald, it's Jennifer, your sister-in-law, don't you remember?"

"Whadda you want? Don't you know what time it is?"

"Well, yes, it's nine-forty. Did you want to know why I called? I was going to tell you when I'd be in Tucson, but if this isn't a good time..."

"Goddammit, Jennifer, it's almost one in the morning!"

"Oh, sorry, I didn't know, I guess I figured the time zones backwards..."

"Are you really that stupid?"

"Oh, well no need to get nasty, just tell me when would be a good time to call?"

"Just tell me now!"

"Okay, I have some good friends who would just love to visit southern Arizona; I want to take them to Tombstone..."

"Get to the fucking point! It's almost ONE AM! When are you going to be there?"

"Well, there's a guest ranch only a short distance from the house, so I'm going to book them in there..."

"GET TO THE POINT!"

I was enjoying this. "Donald, I'm trying to, if you'll just quit interrupting. Anyway, they're going to be at this guest ranch." I gave him the name, address and phone number. "So you may as well get yourself a room there, I might not have time to meet you anywhere else."

"For God's sake, WHEN?"

"Oh, sorry, next weekend. I'll have to get over there Friday so I can go to the credit union to get your papers, so you call them and reserve a room for yourself and I'll meet you there to return your papers. I probably won't have much spare time after my friends get there, so be sure you're there by Friday afternoon."

"I'll have to check my schedule; I can't just drop everything to suit your convenience."

"Suit yourself; I don't know when I'll be able to get over there again."

"If I can't make it I'll send one of my people."

"They have trail rides if your people like horseback riding, but I won't hand those papers over to anyone except you, so come alone. Just let me know if you can make it. Goodnight, Donald, sleep well." I disconnected before he had a chance to say anything else.

I slept very well, and in the morning I called Alex's cell phone before breakfast to tell him about the conversation.

"Jennifer, lass, I never realized you were so devious."

"Well, I wouldn't have wanted to try it face to face, it was all I could do to keep a straight face and a laugh out of my voice."

"As I've told you for years, you don't have a poker face, but I would have loved to listen in on your conversation."

"Damaris told me we should take video of the take down and arrest."

"I'll see if we can equip Stanley for that job; Sam and I will back up Gabriel since it's likely Donald will arrive with backup of his own."

CHAPTER TWENTY-SEVEN
(January 15 – January 16)

Alex's flight would arrive late morning. Sam and Stanley would arrive in Tucson tomorrow afternoon.

"We're cutting it close if anything goes wrong on our way over. I gave Sam an extra key just in case of emergency and if she had to let them in early I told her to call Augie and Gabriel before someone arrived to arrest them."

"What do you expect to go wrong?"

"Nothing, don't worry, but there could be another drunk on board who could have my flight returned to the gate, or some malfunction that diverts the flight and slows my arrival."

"Are we planning to drive all night?"

"I thought we'd stop at that nice campground in Wellton and have a chance to have a swim."

"Alex, it's January! Who in their right mind would go for a swim?"

"Snowbirds who don't get many chances to swim in January. I told both of them to be sure to pack swim suits for the guest ranch pool."

"Surely you don't plan to stage this take down around the pool."

"Noo, we're probably all at our best when we're dressed, but if they want to go home and tell everyone they spent an afternoon in the swimming pool in Arizona, we'll give them the opportunity."

When I met him at the airport – on time – we went back to the house to finish loading up the little motor home. We would deliver the dogs: Monty and Dragon and Misty and her puppies, to Bonnie on the way when we left.

I gave Bonnie the phone number at the resort as well as Sam and Stanley's cell numbers. "Just in case you have to reach us for any reason, but this time no one wants to kidnap the pups, just get their hands on those papers they want back."

"I told Dan what you were doing and he had an idea to send backup for you. He told his old pal, Mike, about it. Mike said since the supposed crime crossed state lines, the FBI could get involved, and there was nothing better he'd like to do than to take down a crooked politician."

"As I recall, good old Mikey didn't exactly cover himself with glory the last couple of times he helped us out," Alex observed.

"Yeah, I know, but he said it might help to have someone with federal jurisdiction even if Mike did trip over his own feet again. Don't you dare tell him Dan said that!"

His idea to stop at the campground was a heavenly break in a long, boring and hot drive. 'Hot' was a relative term in January, but it was definitely warm enough for me to put on my suit and take a relaxing dip in the pool.

Alex grilled steaks while I microwaved frozen stuffed potatoes. It was already dark when we started cooking, we went to bed early, got up at dawn, and after a quick breakfast we got on the road again.

It was still morning when we pulled into our Tucson driveway. I transferred our clothes and the meal ingredients I had packed for us to the house. Our guests weren't due to arrive until mid-afternoon so I had time to run to the Safeway for whatever we still needed for meals. Alex made our phone calls to our neighbor and the deputy who – we hoped – would make the arrest. He also called the guest ranch to let them know we had arrived and would be checking in as soon as the rest of our party landed. We had booked one of their Casas – lodgings that could accommodate up to six persons – and while we planned to have the Wongs stay with us at the house, if we checked in all four of us then we could take advantage of all the amenities of the resort. Since we had our own herd of horses up north, we wouldn't be doing their trail rides, and maybe not the nature walks, but we would certainly all take advantage of the pool at least once, and possibly have a meal in their dining room while we fine-tuned our plotting.

We hadn't reckoned with Sam. "Oh my God, Alex, I've never stayed in any place this luxurious. I know we're supposed to stay with you, but can we stay here at least for one day?"

"Of course; that might make you an even more credible prop. Let's check you in, we checked in earlier by phone since Jennifer and I also have to have free access to the place. We'll take you back to the house for supper and get out our extra vehicle for you to take back there tonight."

When we pulled in we noticed a pall of smoke to the east of the resort. "What's the cause of the smoke?" Alex asked the desk clerk.

"Nothing to worry about, sir, there's just a small brush fire over Reddington Pass. The wind is blowing the opposite direction; it won't affect your stay here." He handed us maps of the grounds and buildings. "And here's your parking area."

"I'll ask Gabriel for more information when we see him," Alex said. "I don't think any brush fire is something to take lightly."

"I agree; some of Arizona's largest fires could have been put out with a few buckets of water when they first started."

The Casa we had booked was part way down a short road and almost as private as our secluded Tucson home. We helped them move their luggage into the spacious guest building. "We still have our own swim suits in the motor home," I told them. "Does anyone want a dip in the pool before we go back to the house?"

"Oh, yes!" Sam said, so we went to our separate rooms in the little house and changed. I had large beach towels in the storage compartments of the motor home, but the resort had supplied huge bath sheets for us to dry off, so we gathered them up for the walk down to the pool. It was tenth of a mile, an easy stroll now, but in summer the heat on the pavement could be uncomfortable, even through our shoes.

The sun was starting to set in a spectacular, fiery display and we went back to the Casa, dressed again, and took Sam and Stanley to the house. While I started our dinner, Alex called Gabriel to ask him to come here and discuss our plans.

I got out the artist's drawings of Donald's pair of goons, and the campaign poster our friend in Atlanta had emailed to us. "You may want to take these back with you so you'll recognize them if you see any of them around the resort."

"Excellent idea," Stanley said, "but maybe we should just copy them to our phones so we don't risk the wrong people seeing them."

"Aye," Alex added, "we probably don't want a motel maid coming across those photos that look exactly like police artist drawings, and recognizing them as guests on the grounds."

"Don't forget how much help Señora Covarrubias was at our

Tucson National,"

"I won't, but I hope we can handle this without involving the resort staff. Unless, of course, there's another kitchen meltdown or we need help getting another DNA sample."

"Well, we don't need that this time."

"True; we also shouldn't leave their pictures lying around, or concealed where someone might wonder why they were hidden."

When Gabe arrived we showed him the documents I had discovered in my nightstand. "This is what Donald is coming to town to retrieve. The contents seem to be evidence that someone would stop at nothing to get the permit for that development. These are copies; I left the originals in my safe deposit box in El Cajon."

"He'll probably be able to figure out that these are copies," Sam told us.

"I'm not sure he's as observant as our forensic experts," I told him, "but the main purpose of holding out these documents is to get him to take the bait. If he brings either of those other goons to town, Gabe has enough evidence to arrest them as well."

"I'm not sure we have enough to actually charge your brother-in-law," Gabe said.

"Just the threat of being touched by scandal may be enough to keep him in line."

"Aye, the threat of this being made public might be enough to keep him to a straight and narrow path," Alex added, "but we may have an added member of our team; an FBI agent who can bring all the jurisdiction we need, with access to resources that we don't have. On a different subject, Gabe, what can you tell us of the brush fire burning to the east of the guest ranch? The man at the desk shrugged it off as, 'Not to worry,' but I think most of us have experience of small brush fires that suddenly become large and deadly."

"We certainly do here; two of the largest in the state were started by humans, and small enough at the start that they could have been stamped out. This one is out near Tanque Verde Falls, on the road to Reddington Pass. As long as the wind keeps blowing from the west it shouldn't be a threat to the city. It was started in just about the stupidest way you can imagine. A guy with one of the law enforcement agencies – thankfully not mine – took a bunch of buddies up toward the pass where's there's so much wildcat shooting that it's a wonder someone isn't killed every weekend. His wife was expecting a baby, so they drove up with their guns and their coolers full of beer, and he led off the party by firing at a highly explosive target full of blue powder. It's at a few thousand acres now and nowhere near containment. This isn't normally what we consider fire season, but our fall and winter rains have been so far under normal that every bit of brush is as dry as tinder. It shouldn't interfere with our plan, but we don't want to take it for granted. By the way, what is our plan?"

"I'm not sure we have one yet. I told Donald I would get here tomorrow so I could get the documents from my safe deposit box. He doesn't know that the originals are actually in my box back in San Diego. I expect the phone to start ringing early tomorrow."

"Jennifer, Alex, I wish I'd thought of this sooner, but it's not too late to put a tap on your phone. I can be back here in less than an hour to hook it up. Meanwhile, all of you use your cell phones for any communications you don't want recorded."

Gabe left, planning to return with the phone recording equipment, I served our dinner and then, before Sam and Stanley left in the Armada to go back to the resort Sam volunteered, "We could stay until your deputy comes back to wire you up,"

"No need, he should be back before our bedtime."

"Well then, we'll help wash up and then leave."

"When you park the Armada, back it in," Alex told them. "Arizona only issues rear license plates. Donald doesn't know what it looks like and there's no reason to give him any help."

Gabe had the phone tap in place in just a few minutes while we watched enough of the late news to catch the weather forecast. It wasn't encouraging: "We're expecting strong winds tomorrow as a front passes through. This is what's known as a back-door front with winds shifting and coming from the east and a drop in temperature. It may also bring smoke from the Saddle Pass fire into the metro area; those with breathing difficulties should take precautions."

"Let's hope that doesn't throw a crimp into our plans," Alex observed as we turned out the lights.

CHAPTER TWENTY-EIGHT
(*Friday, January 17*)

It was still dark when the phone rang in the morning. I was tangled in the bedding with Alex's arm around me, and as I struggled to sit up his arm tightened. "Noo, let it be lass, let the answering machine and Gabe's recording equipment pick it up."

"Dammit, I'm awake now!"

"Then I have a far better use for our time. Remember, you're only supposed to arrive today, so we'll wait to return his call, or calls; I have no doubt they'll be coming in regularly."

We heard the phone ring three more times before we finally got out of bed and showered. It rang again while Alex was in the shower. "Alex, how long do you want me to ignore his calls?"

"At least until well after breakfast. If you're itching for something to keep you occupied, look up the first flight arriving from San Diego today and add most of an hour to collect luggage and take the shuttle. There may be someone in your brother-in-law's entourage with a little more attention to detail than his own."

We were eating stuffed French toast with fresh raspberries and blueberries when the phone rang yet again. This time I could walk around the corner of a wall and hear the message. "Goddammit, Jennifer, you said you'd be here today! Answer this phone or call me back!"

"What's your best arrival time, lass?"

"Leaving San Diego at 8:15, arriving here at 9:30."

"Then we'll start answering his calls after 10:00."

When the phone rang again at five minutes to ten I finally couldn't stand it any longer. Never one to waste time on pleasantries, Donald got right to the point. "Goddammit, Jennifer I've been here since last night. We'll be right over to collect my papers."

"No you won't. I told you that you weren't welcome at our house again, and whoever your companion is, I'm not having one of your bullies come here and push me around again. We'll meet in public at the resort. I just got in, I need time to unpack and go to the credit union to retrieve your documents. I'll meet you at the resort in two hours. What's your room number?"

I repeated the number back to him and Alex wrote it down. When I ended the call from Donald, Alex got out his own phone and called Dan. "Detective Dan, is Mike actually planning to be here today? He is? Well then, here's the room number for Jennifer's brother-in-law. Does he have our cell numbers? Aye, that's a good idea, let me write it down. Tell him not to call the house phone, Jennifer is supposed to be here on her own and has errands to run that will keep her out of the house so we don't want Donald to get a busy signal when no one should be here." He disconnected. "Jennifer, Mikey is already checked in at the ranch. Dan will call him with Donald's room number, and we'll call him when we're ready to head out there."

I opened my own phone and called Sam's number. "Sam, Donald called, several times, actually, and I told him I'd be there in about two hours. Here's his room number so you can keep your eyes open for him. And Dan's FBI buddy is also there, apparently in a room just two or three removed from Donald's."

"Okay, we'll keep one eye tilted toward those rooms. It's a good thing we had our swim yesterday, it's cold this morning. Up home we'd wonder about snow."

"Not much chance of that as dry as it's been, but we do have a cold front moving in and it's coming from the east, so there was a caution about smoke."

"Yeah, it's blowing back this way this morning and the air is kind of murky. That won't mess up our plans, will it?"

"I don't think so. I'll call when we're ready to leave here."

At 11:30 I called Sam and told her we were on our way. "Tuck yourselves into one of the rooms until we see if we need you."

Alex moved out of sight to the sofa in the back while I started the motor home. He opened his phone and called Mike. "Yes, we're on our way. Oh, excellent idea, where? I'll call our deputy and have him meet us there as well. Do you have enough equipment to wire him as well? Very good." He closed the phone. "Jennifer, we're to meet Mike in the large parking area near the check-in desk. He's going to wire us up so he'll be able to hear every bit of conversation that goes on." He passed the information along to Gabe and in a few minutes we all met in the large parking lot. We followed Mike to the far edge of the lot where a few thick mesquite trees hid us from view.

I hardly recognized Gabe; his pickup truck looked even older with a coating of mud and dust. "I drove it up a couple of dirt trails to give it this look," and he was dressed in a plaid flannel western shirt with cowboy hat and boots, and a hay bale in the bed of his truck. He looked exactly like one of the ranch's horse wranglers. "That's the whole idea," he said with a grin.

Mike fitted each of us with a tiny, hidden microphone. "All of these feed to mine. You can't talk to each other, but I can relay information to all three of you."

Mike had also downloaded and printed the map of the resort grounds. "Your friends with the Armada are parked down here," he indicated a small parking area just adjacent to our hacienda, "and I'll be parked up here," he indicated a arger area near the building where he and Donald had their rooms. "My room is high enough that I can see your lot and your building. If things start happening I can be down there in seconds."

"Where's Donald's room?"

He pointed to a number printed on the building, "That's his, mine is here three rooms down."

"Any activity at his?"

"Not that I've seen. I've been strolling around with binoculars trying to look like a birdwatcher. I'll drive down to my place now; you follow in a few minutes."

I did, with Alex muttering from the rear, "Some birdwatcher, have you noticed that we haven't seen a single bird? The vultures and hawks have all gone south, cactus wrens and other SBB's are about all that's left."

"SBB's?"

"Small, brown birds."

I parked a couple of spaces away from the Armada, and I also backed in. Donald knew what this vehicle looked like, but I wanted to be ready in case some fast action was required. I was barely two vehicle lengths away from our patio if we needed backup from Sam and Stanley.

Donald's packet of papers was tucked away in a kitchen drawer in the motor home. I walked up to our hacienda and let myself in and then called Donald's room from our room phone. I didn't want to call on my cell and have it give away my own number; I'd already replaced one phone to keep my personal number out of my family's hands.

Donald was just as pleasant as I expected. "Goddammit, Jennifer, it's about time! I've interrupted my busy schedule to accommodate you."

"Welcome to Tucson, Donald, now go home! If you're going to be rude you can just leave now."

"Just get my papers and I'll leave."

"They're in the motor home. You know what it looks like, meet me over there."

Sam followed me out to the patio and settled down in a chair with a book. "I'll just be ready in case I have to make another flying tackle."

"You may want to turn the book over; you're holding it upside down."

I expected Donald to walk down to meet me but instead what looked like a rental sedan pulled out from the upper parking area, down to ours, and parked in front of my motor home – effectively blocking it in. I hadn't planned on making a getaway myself so it was just an act of pettiness, or a show of control. Control, apparently, when his goon got out of the driver's side. "I told Donald to come alone."

"Yo, Cupcake, no one tells our congressman what to do. Where's those papers?"

"They're inside."

"Let's just go inside and get them."

"You're not coming inside."

"Donny boy, get out here and get those papers for us."

Donald got out of the passenger side, started toward me and then stopped. "What's that? Is it an alligator?"

I looked where he was pointing and it was a very large Gila monster, sunning itself on the warm gravel. "Donald, don't step on it…"

"Donny, kick the goddamned thing out of your way and get over here."

Donald kicked at it with his left foot, but the lizard was quicker. It whipped its head around and sunk its teeth into his shoe. Donald screamed and hopped backwards. "Get it off of me! Jennifer, pull it off!"

"Donald, very carefully pull your foot out of your shoe and back away."

"Goddammit, these are two hundred dollar shoes!"

"If you do as I say you'll still have a hundred dollar half of the pair. Donald, they're venomous. When it chews through your shoe it will start on your foot. Do as I say."

He shook his foot and the lizard bit down harder. "Get it off! Dwayne, shoot it or something."

"They're also protected; if you harm it you can spend six months in jail."

Dwayne was losing his patience. He grabbed my arm, "C'mon, Cupcake, let's get in there and get my papers."

His papers? "I said you're not going inside with me."

"Who's going to stop me?"

"I guess that would be me again," my husband said, stepping down from the motor home holding the envelope. "You've put your hands on my wife too many times already."

Dwayne let go of my arm, grabbed the envelope from Alex and spun around. "Donny, shake off the shoe and let's go." Donald finally did. By then he had danced and hopped his way several feet behind the sedan. Dwayne charged after him, grabbed his shirt and yelled, "Get in the car, you stupid twat!"

"Ow, I can't, I can't walk on this gravel without my shoe."

Dwayne propelled him, still yelling, into the passenger seat and ran to the driver's side. As he started the engine I heard Mike's voice in my hidden earpiece. "Gabe, he's moving, block the exit road," as Dwayne gunned the engine and took off. Donald's door swung shut but didn't quite latch.

I saw Sam running toward us. Stanley followed her, with video running, to where Alex and I were standing, watching the Gila monster still chewing on Donald's shoe. "What a monster! Is that what I think it is?" Sam asked.

"*Heloderma suspectum*," Stanley answered. "A Gila monster."

"I didn't think they got that big. I've only seen pictures and they looked much smaller. It's as long as two of those shoes! Are they really poisonous?"

"Venomous, my dear, not fatally for humans, but I've heard the bite is painful enough that someone bitten might wish he was dead."

I added, "I've heard that ninety percent of bite victims that go to the hospital still have the lizard attached. They just hang on and keep chewing."

Alex joined in, "When we were touring Tombstone I read a few lines from an old newspaper that suggested that the animals are so sluggish that the victim has to help in order to get bitten."

"Donald certainly did. Do you suppose he'll want his shoe

back?" While we were all taking pictures with our phones – from a discreet distance – the creature had finally decided there was no further threat from the expensive suede moccasin and waddled back into the brush at the edge of the parking area.

Meanwhile, Dwayne and Donald were making their getaway. Mike described what happened next: Gabe had moved his truck to a narrow spot on the exit road that should have stopped Dwayne's escape, but there was a dirt track that cut off and went up a short hill to connect with the dirt road over Reddington Pass. The smoke from the fire had been blown back toward town and had created enough haze in the air that it wasn't obvious when they reached the road, which way town was. Dwayne made the wrong choice.

Dwayne turned to the right, away from the city and stepped on the gas again. Partway up the hill on the dirt road the little sedan's wheels began to slip and it slewed sideways. He regained control and gained the crest of the hill, at which point he came to a stop, the passenger side door flew open and Donald tumbled out onto the road.

Gabe and Mike both had to stop or they'd have run over him – not that I would have minded. Mike had a four-wheel-drive vehicle borrowed from the local FBI office. It wasn't a 'cage car' as used by the police, but the back doors could be locked remotely. He grabbed Donald and hauled him to the vehicle, "Still yelling that he couldn't walk on the rocky ground," Mike reported. "He was screaming that his arm was broken too."

Gabe continued the pursuit for a few more minutes and then turned around and headed back down.

We had all piled into the motor home, with Alex driving, and followed the cloud of dust until we caught up with Mike and Gabe. They walked over to meet us, and we heard Donald yelling from the back of Mike's SUV. "Hey, let me out of here! Let me out."

Sam walked over to the SUV and glanced inside. "You guys, he's trying to climb over the front seat."

Mike hustled over there, "Yo, Roth, I'm doing you a favor by not handcuffing you, but if you don't just sit back down there, I will. You're under arrest by the FBI."

"You can't do that. I'm a congressman."

"I already have, now shut up!"

When he came back he asked Gabe, "Why'd you let him get away?"

"I didn't. He didn't. When we got over the crest of the hill the fire had burned up to the road and jumped it and there was a fire truck blocking the road. One of the fire fighters tried to wave him off but he kept going. The smoke was thick, I think he got disoriented; he turned right, away from the fire, and went over a drop-off maybe a hundred yards off the road. I know how far that drop is; we've had to do search and rescue out here. If he survived it would be a miracle, but I wasn't going to try to climb down there in a fire."

"What about those precious papers?" Mike asked. "Do you think those can be retrieved?"

I laughed. "Mike, there are so many copies of those papers floating around that theirs will never be missed. The originals are in my safe deposit box in San Diego. If you can figure out who should take possession of them I'll be happy to turn them over."

CHAPTER TWENTY-NINE
(*January 18 – January 20*)

We spent a day with Sam and Stanley in Tombstone and by the time we left Tucson, Mike had called to tell us that a search and rescue crew had confirmed that Dwayne was indeed deceased and that they had thoroughly questioned Donald and finally released him.

"I'm sorry to have to tell you this, but we didn't have any evidence that he actually had any role in the fatal arson."

"But Donald bought the siding panels that helped fuel the fire."

"Yes, but apparently the credit card was issued by the lobbying organization that sent him out there and other personnel of the organization had access to the company card. He said Dwayne borrowed the card from him, and the signature on the receipt doesn't quite look like Roth's."

"When he was confronted with the fact that he apparently bought the siding panels he tried to say I asked him to buy them for me. I had to get printouts of my phone records in case I had to defend myself."

"Now he's denying he ever said that and claiming you have an overactive imagination."

"You should have run over him instead of stopping!"

"We do have a few other people to investigate. So far, your brother-in-law is stupid and an asshole, neither of which is a federal offence. If we have to toss him back, we still may catch bigger fish. However, you'll be happy to hear that he has a broken collarbone and two broken fingers, on opposite sides, so he has his right arm in a sling and two fingers splinted on his left hand, and he can't even scratch his ass if it itches."

I didn't even want to think about that picture. "Did you retrieve those papers he wanted so badly?"

"The envelope had fallen out of the car so I don't know if he got everything back. Naturally we had a good look at them first."

"Remember, I have the originals, and I scanned them so I can send you anything you're missing."

"Keep them safe until we figure out where they should go."

We got home late Tuesday morning and I called Bonnie to let her know we could pick up the dogs.

"If you want to feed us we can bring them back after I feed the kennel later."

"It's a deal, and we'll tell you the whole story."

I made a simple casserole and as we ate Alex and I took turns telling the tale.

"You know what's missing?" Bonnie asked. "One of your dogs has come to the rescue every time you've been in trouble before. This time you left them all home."

"This time we had another guardian angel. Show them, Alex."

Alex played the forty-second video of the monster chewing on Donald's shoe and finally shuffling away into the brush.

Epilogue
(February)

It was several weeks later. Alex was down now to go to the Silver Bay shows with me. We had invited Dan and Bonnie, and Marcus of course, for dinner tonight; we had interesting news for them. A letter had come from our friends in Atlanta, the District Attorney Forrest Willoughby, and his wife Muriel, with three clippings enclosed.

Washington Lobbyist Investigated in Arizona Deaths.
Lobbyist Lawrence DeLuca is under nvestigation
in two Arizona deaths late last year, and a third
in Tucson last month." The article went on to
summarize the deaths of Bryce and Janet Webb,
the investigation into the arson fire, and the
death of Dwayne Maguirk while in Arizona on
an assignment for DeLuca.

**Cabinet Secretary Resigns in Allegations
Of Pressure on Arizona Official**
It named the Secretary accused of pressure to force the
issuance of a critical permit while enjoying the
hospitality of the developer trying to build a major
housing project in a small Arizona town.

The third clipping was from an Atlanta daily paper:

Newly Seated Congressman Takes Leave of Absence
Congressman Donald Roth, elected in November
and seated in January of this year has taken a
leave of absence, citing previously undiagnosed
health problems in a family member.

And finally, an email from Augie with a scanned newspaper clipping attached:

Developer scraps Tuscan Villas Project

A spokesman for Sunnyskies Builders told reporters, "We're dropping the Tuscan Villas venture, it's just too hard to get any local support. We're bidding on vacant federal land near Apache Junction instead."

Author's Notes

I was working on the final chapters when I realized that while most of the other books have one of our dogs saving the day, this time we'd left them all back in San Diego. What to do? Those flashes of brilliance that occur at 3:00 AM when you can't get back to sleep rarely stand the test of daylight. This one did, so the dogs had a stunt double in this plot.

The Gila monster is an icon of the southwestern desert with a surly temperament. There has never been a human death attributed to its bite, but those bitten have been heard to say that they wished they could die. It is said that ninety percent of those who go to the hospital for a Gila monster bite still have the animal attached to their hand or finger. Many unfortunate victims have been Good Samaritans who tried to scoop one out of the swimming pool with their fingers. Like the rattlesnake and the scorpion, the Gila monster has no sense of gratitude; if you annoy it, it will bite you.

I've been lucky enough to see three of them in the wild in my lifetime: one at Lake Havasu long ago on a fishing trip with my Dad, one when I took Marilyn to the Boyce Thompson Arboretum east of Phoenix, and this beauty found basking in the sun in our own driveway. The prickly pear pads in the background measure about 9" – 10" so we estimated its size at pretty close to 22" – 24" the top end of its size range.

Yes, Grand Marnier really can go up in a fireball in the kitchen; we proved it.

Finally, there is a massive housing development under consideration in the small town of Benson, east of Tucson. Our local paper, and even a national cable news channel, carried the story of a federal employee being pressured to change his decision on a key permit. I'm happy to report that the official is very much alive and retired, but the story made a good springboard for a mystery.

Karen Harbert is a successful breeder and exhibitor of Cardigan Welsh Corgis with about one hundred championships to her credit. She has served multiple terms on the Board of Directors of the Cardigan Welsh Corgi Club of America; she has been president of two regional Cardigan clubs and editor of national and regional club magazines. She has judged Sweepstakes at a National Specialty in Canada and at a National Club supported show in the US. She is a member of the Board of Directors of the Dog Writers Association of America.

At the 2019 CWCCA National Spec alty, Karen was named an Honorary Lifetime Member, 'In recognition for long service and dedication.'

Professionally, Karen held management positions in mental health, adult protective services and child protective services.

More by This Author

FINAL ENTRY

Jennifer Brooks is administrator of a mental health program as well as a breeder and exhibitor of Cardigan Welsh Corgis, and Board member of the national club. The club's treasurer, Edith, is killed and her husband asks Jennifer to take Edith's dogs and club records. The husband's house is robbed. That break-in is followed by attempts at Jennifer's office and her home but there her faithful show dog Monty keeps the thief out.

When Jennifer flies east to the national board meeting her home is burglarized. A clue is found that has Jennifer following its trail to San Francisco and back. She finds the records that Edith was killed for and brings the murderer to her own front door.

FALSE PAPERS

Is a bad job of judging dogs grounds for murder? Dog show judges are being killed and Jennifer has to figure out why before she becomes a victim. Monty's devotion as well as his obedience training get Jennifer out of a dangerous situation.

DEATH MARCH

Jennifer and her boyfriend, Kent, rent a motor home to go to the dog show circuit known as the Oregon Death March. Supposedly for the weather, but accidents keep happening to people and dogs along the way. RCMP Inspector Alexander MacLeod is another exhibitor on the circuit and when Jennifer is drugged and dumped in the path of a forest fire, Monty leads rescuers to her and Alex helps solve the mystery.

BRAT PACK

Teenage Sabrina witnesses what could be an attempted molestation in a dark building on the Yuma fairgrounds. She and Jennifer decide to keep an eye on the junior handlers to see if they can figure it out. Another incident convinces Jennifer that a pedophile is preying on youngsters. Meanwhile, accidents have been happening to some of the top winning junior handlers. Sabrina sets up a sting and everything that can go wrong does.

OH CANADA

Jennifer and friends go to Canada for a show circuit at the invitation of Inspector MacLeod. A shot is fired at Jennifer and Alex on a horseback ride and then an attempt is made to poison the dogs. Sabrina, now set on a forensics career, manages to get the fingerprints of the suspected bad guy and as they figure out the villain and motive Alex rescues Jennifer from a burning barn.

PUPSICLES

Jennifer and Kent plan to breed his champion, Heather Mary, to a top winning English import but the 10 year old dog is apparently sterile. Jen's best friend owns frozen semen and Jennifer flies back east with the female. A troubling character has been trying to get his hands on that frozen semen and attempts to kidnap Heather Mary, then later the litter. When the pups are old enough Jennifer and Kent take them to the national specialty to turn them over to their new owners. The fellow that Jennifer suspects suffers from megalomania kidnaps the entire litter and holds Jennifer hostage at knife point to get her to sign them over.

CALCULATED RISK

Jen and her friend Barb are trying to contact the club president, who is also the club's insurance agent, after a child was bitten at the national specialty. He won't return calls, his wife dies in a freak accident and he's 'in seclusion.' A nasty woman connected with his family tries to sabotage other exhibitors so that her dog can win.

Jennifer is bored, and suspicious, and starts investigating other clubs who use her club's president as their insurance agent, with disquieting results.

Sabrina and Jerry are now married and have moved to Oregon. Jennifer, Kent and Alex MacLeod go to a dog show there to see the kids again and they run into the president and the nasty woman who turns out to be his lover. She pulls a gun, Jerry and Sabrina save the day.

FLASH FLOOD

Tragedy strikes and Jennifer's friends conspire to bring happiness back into her life with surprising results. A mysterious murder in Canada leads to a disappearance in San Diego. A corrupt politician with ties to a professional handler is somehow involved and when Jennifer figures out the connection she's almost drowned in a flash flood. As always, Monty comes to the rescue.

A WALK ON THE WILD SIDE

A serial killer is stalking the dog show circuit. When a friend of Sabrina's is a victim she insists Detective Dan and Alex MacLeod have to solve it. And then she designs a sting where, of course, whatever can go wrong does.

FIFTEEN SHADES OF MERLE

Someone is selling dogs of disqualified colors as show quality. She has mysteriously acquired a daughter of Jen's beloved Monty. When Alex

MacLeod connives to buy the dog they earn the enmity of the duped owner and the person who sold the dog to her. From a shootout in Arizona to a canoe trip in eastern Canada, to a blizzard in Alberta, they'll stop at nothing to keep Jennifer from regaining possession of Monty's daughter.

JUST DESERT

A spur of the moment camping trip and chance encounter with an elderly couple start a bizarre set of circumstances in motion. Monty leads Jennifer and Alex to a concealed desert encampment at the end of an abandoned runway. The actions of a deputy sheriff and the campground owner arouse their suspicions.

Meanwhile, Jennifer and her boss are trying to figure out how to trap the employee who is ripping off large quantities of office supplies. While they work to plan a sting, the elderly friends are nearly killed and solving the desert mystery becomes a priority.

Sabrina and Jerry devise a sting for the desert operation, which, naturally, goes wrong.

UNDER THE TUCSON SUN

A pair of outsiders are running for office in the national club and trying to smear Jennifer's friends. Sabrina helps unearth a long-ago scandal concerning the candidates so they turn their wrath on Jennifer and fellow Board member Barb Neville, accusing them of substituting dogs in the show ring – a violation than could ban them for life. At the national specialty in Tucson, Alex helps arrest an attempted murderer, which sends the other killer after Jennifer, and it ends with the perfect sting.

DOG-TAGGED

Vandals are attacking show dogs, exhibitors and equipment with cans of spray paint and paintball guns, and setting dogs loose at shows. Is it

Animal Rights activists, or something more sinister? When Sabrina gets involved the vandalism takes a deadly turn.

MARITIME SUMMER
2018 DWAA Maxwell Award Finalist

An idyllic vacation in Canada's Maritime Provinces turns deadly when fraud and forgery are uncovered. The perpetrator locks Jennifer and Jamie, her nine-year-old nephew, in an abandoned farmhouse and sets the house on fire. Clever Jamie figures out how to escape.

MEDIUM RARE
2018 DWAA Maxwell Award Finalist

A knife-happy veterinarian performs unnecessary surgeries to fuel an expensive hobby. If his patients don't survive, he has a friend – a Pet Grief Therapist – who is also a 'Certified Animal Medium,' and can contact your deceased pet in the afterlife. For a fee, naturally. When an elderly relative of Jennifer's friend has been taken for thousands of dollars, Jennifer decides to investigate.

SOUTHERN DISCOMFORT

"You've met my family, now it's time for me to meet yours," Alex tells Jennifer. The National Specialty is in Atlanta, where Jennifer's mother, and sister and family live. But Jennifer's mother refuses to meet Alex so he joins her, incognito, at a formal event given by her family's 'spiritual advisor.' Jennifer's brother-in-law announces his candidacy for national office and suggests that Jennifer's marriage to a 'foreigner' could put his campaign at risk. The 'spiritual advisor' concocts a plan to end Jennifer's marriage and gain control of her assets for himself.

JUDGMENT

Jennifer's assignment to computerize an inefficient set of file cards and a friend's request to do a welfare check on a retired dog show judge become part of the same problem when it appears that the clients of a few home health aides are dying – and leaving their property to those same aides.

CROOK'D

Sheep are sweet and gentle creatures, Right? Maybe not. Jennifer and Alex help the club out as volunteers at a herding trial where their champion Cardigans try the herding instinct test. Jennifer suspects that times are being manipulated in the actual trial to favor certain contestants. They decide to follow up at a later trial where they find themselves involved in solving one murder and preventing another - with the help of her young dog's newly discovered herding ability.

DINNER AT THE DOG SHOW

A work in progress. Several readers expressed interest in Jennifer's recipes, so Marilyn, Pat and I decided to cook them, photograph them, and put them together as a companion volume. It grew so quickly that when I tried to compile it, it overpowered my word processing program and crashed. My solution was to put it on a CD.

If you cooks out there would like to try the dishes that made you drool, send me an email for information on how to get it. It has another fabulous cover by Jean Clifford: Three Cardigans resembling the three witches in *Macbeth*, stirring a boiling cauldron filled with rats, eyeballs, an octopus or two as well as toads and fishes. It's enough to curdle your appetite.

Dinner at the Dog Show
A companion to Murder at the Dog Show
KAREN HARBERT

www.ingramcontent.com/pod-product-compliance
Lightning Source LLC
Chambersburg PA
CBHW020954160726
47994CB00006B/2216